Gone With THE WOLF

a *Seattle Wolf Pack* novel

Kristin Miller

This book is a work of fiction. Names, characters, places, and incidents are the product of the author's imagination or are used fictitiously. Any resemblance to actual events, locales, or persons, living or dead, is coincidental.

Copyright © 2013 by Kristin Miller. All rights reserved, including the right to reproduce, distribute, or transmit in any form or by any means. For information regarding subsidiary rights, please contact the Publisher.

Entangled Publishing, LLC
2614 South Timberline Road
Suite 109
Fort Collins, CO 80525
Visit our website at www.entangledpublishing.com.

Covet is an imprint of Entangled Publishing, LLC.

Edited by Liz Pelletier and Kaleen Harding
Cover design by Curtis Svehlak
Cover art from iStock

Manufactured in the United States of America

First Edition April 2013

Covet

For Justin, always.

Chapter One

Emelia Hudson knew she shouldn't be snooping through her boss's wine cellar, but his secret stash was down here and damn it, he owed her a bottle. Or a case.

Slipping off her heels, Emelia kicked them into the corner of the spacious cellar, and jumped from the feel of the frosty granite floor against her bare feet. The cellar was bigger than her Seattle apartment, with a nasty draft sweeping through the wrought iron French doors behind her. The space felt more like a high-class smoking room than a cellar, with large stone pillars, leather-wrapped seats, and a pungent musk floating in the air. Chandeliers hung on either end of the ceiling, shedding amber auras of light over two barrels topped with stone slabs. Not a single wine case cluttered the floor, and not a single pigeonhole was deprived of a bottle.

"There you are, beautiful," Emelia said, swiping a corked bottle of 1996 Château Lafite off one of the barrels.

She refilled her glass—for the fifth time this evening—and swirled the dark liquid round and round. The mint and black currant aroma hit her nose, causing her eyes to roll back in her head. Taking a sip, Emelia moaned as the bold flavor of succulent silk hit her tongue.

"You," she said, pinching her eyes shut, savoring the changing flavors, "are simply divine."

"I'll say," someone said from the doorway.

Emelia started. Droplets of wine hurtled down her throat, catching like stones in her windpipe. She choked hard and bowled over as she tried to the get the damn silky stuff out of her lungs.

"That good, huh?" The man was beside her before she knew what was happening, massaging small circles across her back.

Emelia backed against the barrel and away from the stranger's touch. From the few seconds he'd massaged her, Emelia's skin had warmed, tingling with strange, electrically charged sensations.

"I'm fine," she choked out, gaining her bearings.

The stranger radiated intimidation. Six feet tall. Broad, flexing shoulders. His white cotton dress shirt was pulled taut, stretching over layers of rippling muscle. A square, hard-set jaw with a shadow of stubble, and pressed-white lips gave him a downright stony appearance. But despite his hardened expression and daunting stature, mesmerizing chocolate-brown eyes bore into Emelia's, chilling her body to match her bare feet.

Did this guy work for Wilder Financial? Was he a bouncer sent to drag her back upstairs? The Halloween office party had been monster-mashing for the last two hours and the cellar had been deemed off-limits. Solitude was the reason Emelia sought out the cellar in the first place. Well, that and her boss's stash of fine wine.

"No one's supposed to be down here," she said, nerves kicking up a notch.

"I could tell you the same thing." Folding his arms across

his barrel of a chest, the stranger backed away and leaned against the doorframe. A slow smile spread across his full lips. "I don't recall Little Red Riding Hood packing wine on her trip to Grandmother's."

"Yeah, well…" Emelia flicked at the cape brushing her knees and laughed. "I hate costume parties and didn't think I was coming until the last minute. When I finally decided I had to be here, the costume store had two choices: Little Red Riding Slut or Sexy Feather-Dusting Maid. I went with Little Red."

Why'd she just tell him all that? She shouldn't have gulped down that last glass of wine. It had loosened her lips, affecting her more than it should've.

"I think the costume was a good choice." The stranger strode into the cellar, his gait confident and powerful, and swept a thick-stemmed wineglass off the nearest barrel. "May I? Or were you planning on downing that bottle yourself?"

"No, no, please, help yourself." With a tipsy bow and a giggle, Emelia swept her arm aside. "Where's your costume?"

He glanced down at his slacks as if he just realized he wasn't dressed for the party. "Maybe I'm the Big Bad Wolf hiding in business attire instead of old lady pajamas."

"You don't look like a wolf."

"No?"

Emelia leaned in close, squinting at his glinting white — and very human — teeth, then laughed. "Nope. No fangs."

He eyed her curiously, filled his glass, and sipped on it as though he'd never tasted anything like it before. He swished the wine in his cheeks before swallowing, all the while holding Emelia's gaze. Intensity smoldered behind his eyes; Emelia swore someone kicked the thermostat up a few degrees.

"So," he said, eyeing her wild mane of blond hair that'd come loose from her hood, "why do you *have* to be here?"

Although Emelia knew the man wasn't really a wolf—

come on, those only existed in Paris-set horror movies, *Twilight*, and her wildest dreams—he gazed at her like he was insatiably hungry. Her body quivered beneath his gorgeous stare. Stunned by the man's raw sexual appeal, Emelia shook cobwebs from her brain. "Excuse me?"

"You said you hate parties and that you have to be here. Did some crazed date make you come?"

"Oh, if you only knew."

"Enlighten me." He smiled slowly, twinging something in Emelia's chest.

As much as she wanted to tell this stranger the truth, she couldn't.

I'm here to seduce our boss. Chain him to his bed. Take some pictures. Instagram them to the web. You know, the usual Halloween party antics.

Not only would the hot-to-trot stranger laugh in her face, he would probably run to her superiors and blab his brains out, and she would lose her secretarial temp job. She couldn't let that happen. She needed the money, and she needed to figure out a way to talk to Mr. Wilder about the massive wrench he'd thrown in her gears. Two months ago, he claimed to have bought the building that her bar, the Knight Owl, resides in. If she hadn't dumped her savings into the place, she would've hired a lawyer to figure out what was going on and fight back. But under the circumstances, Emelia could barely afford the gas in her car to get to work.

She'd spent weeks trying to get past Wilder Financial's complaint department and kept ramming into a stone wall of indifference. No matter how many letters Emelia sent demanding to set up a meeting with Mr. Wilder, or how many times she called to talk about how it was impossible that they both had a deed to the same building, no one listened. No one cared. Even when she'd tried to bypass Mr. Wilder's flunkies and communicate with him directly, she'd gotten the same response. Mr. Stuck-Up Wilder refused to acknowledge her presence. He always seemed too occupied at his East Coast offices, or unavailable to meet.

So she'd taken a job at his office, hoping to kill two birds with one stone—she'd make some money, and figure out what the hell was going on in the process.

Mr. Wilder wouldn't be able to ignore her once he was good and tied to his bed.

Only that plan had gone down the toilet, along with her hopes and dreams of the Knight Owl becoming the most well-known bar in Seattle. Mr. Wilder had been called away on business and wouldn't be attending the Halloween party after all.

"Guess you could say I was dying to pay back Mr. Wilder for something."

Her words seemed to intrigue the stranger. His dark brows quirked. His shoulders tensed—only a bit—but she noticed. He took a long, hard drink instead of responding, and an uncomfortable silence fizzed between them.

Did she say something wrong? Did he have some vendetta against Mr. Wilder, too? Rumors of Mr. Wilder's coldness preceded him. Maybe his harsh, careless demeanor had permeated through his business more than she'd originally thought. The possibility lessened Emelia's guilt, taking weight off her shoulders—Mr. Wilder deserved what was coming to him.

"You never said what you were doing down here." Emelia tapped her fingers against the stone-topped barrel, wondering if there was another bouncer on the way. And exactly what was the alcohol content of the wine she drank? Her insides were warm and her brain was fuzzy. No wine had ever affected her this way before. "Are you on duty?"

"On duty?" The tension in his shoulders eased as a laugh escaped him. "No, I'm here for the party. I work for Wilder

Financial Services like you do."

"I've never seen you there before." She would've remembered seeing a Greek god wandering the whitewashed halls. Damn, her teeth were beginning to chatter. She would be lucky to remember any of this night. What a disaster. "Which depot—I mean, department, are you in?"

"Administration." He leaned against a stone pillar and pushed his dark hair behind his ears. Why was he acting like he had nowhere to go? Didn't he have to get back up to the party? He'd have a date waiting for him, wouldn't he? Drop-dead gorgeous Channing Tatum look-alikes never came to parties stag. "You?"

"I'm a temp. I started last month as a secretary, but they've already shuffled me 'round to marketing, directory assistance, and main office…*something*." She shooed her hand around her face as the words evaporated from her brain. "I'm more like an office rover than anything. Ha!" She snorted, then caught herself. "I'm Rover. Woof!"

The stranger laughed and seemed to relax into the pillar. "Let me get this straight…you hate costume parties and you hate being here, but since Mr. Wilder isn't coming tonight, you've decided to empty his stash of expensive wine?"

"Pretty much." She nodded. As the thought of Mr. Wilder coming home to his mansion and finding an emptied wine cellar struck her, Emelia laughed, lurched forward, and slapped the stranger in the chest. The instant her hand struck a warm slate of stone, she drew it back and held it against her stomach. "Have you ever met him?"

His brown eyes burned with hints of desire. "Once or twice."

"What's he like?"

"He's a bit of a prick, really. Cold. Controlled. Probably not your type." He frowned at the last part, though he couldn't have known how true he shot. "What's your name?"

She teetered a bit, closer to his tantalizing masculine scent, then farther away. "Emelia Hudson, but friends call me Emie. I'm not usually like this, I swear. I can usually hold my liquor; I'm a bartender for crying out loud. I think it's because I haven't eaten anything today." She squinted, her vision going a bit blurry. What was happening? "I'm starving."

"You're a bartender? I thought you said you were a temp."

"Potato, potahto. Ooh, I could really go for some fries right now." The chandeliers began to tilt and spin as the floor rolled beneath Emelia's feet. She closed the distance between them and stood up on teetering tiptoe to meet him eye to eye. Her skin flushed hot. If the temperature in the cellar hadn't just skyrocketed, she was the first twenty-five-year-old on record to start menopause. "Am I as hot as you are? I mean, are you as hot as I am? No, that's not right either." She paused, slowing her thoughts to molasses. "Is the room spinning for you, too?"

She may have been seeing things, but could've sworn the stranger nodded. "You're not what I was expecting to find when I came down here tonight. You're not afraid to say what's on your mind, are you?"

"Nope." She put her hand to her head, steadying herself. "Never have been."

A strange vibe shot between them as he put two fingers to her chin and lifted her gaze to his.

"There's something about you," he whispered. Emelia felt like a puppet on a string, held captive by the two fingers holding her chin. "You're…different."

"Is diff'rent good?" It had to be the wine. It had to be the hint of want sparking in the stranger's dark, brooding eyes. It had to be the fact that she'd never see him again—Wilder Financial Services was a maze of offices and halls. The urge to taste the stranger's lips overtook her. "What am I doing?"

As the question escaped her lips, Emelia pressed forward, brushing her lips against his.

His mouth was soft and supple. Dreamier than it should've been. Maybe it was the excitement of kissing a stranger. Yup, had to be it. Excitement sizzled through Emelia's body, curling her toes, crinkling the skin over her bones. No one had ever riled her up this much from doing so little. It was a kiss. A tiny little kiss that could've been forgotten.

There was no way she'd forget this. As Emelia parted her lips to draw the stranger's tongue into her mouth, he pulled back.

"We probably shouldn't," he said, but the hunger in his eyes spoke otherwise.

How could he deny her? She'd already tasted the sweetness of his lips and wanted more. As she leaned forward to catch his mouth, she misjudged the distance between them and smashed against his chest. He caught her, roping an arm around her waist.

"Forget me tomorrow. Hell, forget me tonight." Shivers danced over Emelia's skin and she closed her eyes. "But kiss me now."

He squeezed her tightly against him. Crushed his mouth to hers with more passion than she expected. She became drunk on his mouth, his kiss, the way he worked his tongue like a skilled lover. He tasted of wine and lust and intensity unlike anything she'd ever had. She lost herself in him. Felt her body pull to his. She molded against his sculpted chest. Moaned into his mouth and dug her fingers into his hair.

With a growl, he pulled back, keeping her at arm's length, his fingers gouging into her shoulders. "This isn't possible." He breathed hard, chest heaving. "This can't be happening. Not now."

Oh, this was happening. Right here. Right now.

"Where'd you come from?"

God, she was so dizzy. Was she sitting? Lying down? She pinched her eyes shut, willing his mouth to cover hers again. "I come from the Knight Owl."

"What? No, I mean which office are you from? Did someone send you?"

"It's the name of my bar. The Knight Owl. That's why I'm here." She was saying too much. She should stop. She should kiss him again and shut him up, too.

She pushed forward, but he'd already pulled away, dropping his hands from her shoulders. "I'm sorry, Emelia, but I have to go."

Emelia's eyes flashed open and she spun, landing against the massive wine rack with a thud. "I don't even know your name."

Not that she wanted to know. Nope. Didn't want to look him up in the office directory for a night of fun. No way.

"Drake," he said, turning back at the French doors that led out of the cellar. "My friends call me Drake. And I have to say, while you probably won't remember this, you're the sexiest Little Red Riding Hood I've ever seen."

"Isn't Drake the name of a plant from Harry Potter?" Heart thudding in her chest, Emelia closed her eyes and laid her head on the rack behind her. "What was it called again? Drake…miss…mandrake! Yup, that's it. The plant with all the crazy roots."

When Emelia peeled her eyes open, Drake was gone, leaving her with a warm buzz in her belly, a brain as empty as her glass of Lafite, and the lingering taste of their kiss on her tongue.

Chapter Two

As the sun reached its peak in the sky the next day, Drake stepped out of his limo and onto the busy curb in front of Wilder Financial. If he were the nervous type, his palms would've been sticky with sweat. He would've adjusted his tie a thousand times on the ride over. He would've phoned the office to make sure everything was in order. Instead, his body became rigid, wound tight with anticipation. Knots of tension pinballed around his stomach, and his chest hardened with hot rods of adrenaline.

Struggling to keep his impulses in check, Drake strode through the glass doors of his office building and passed by a gawking secretary, who stood the instant he made eye contact.

"Good morning, Mr. Wilder," she said, alarmed, pressing down the front of her dress suit.

"Good morning." Drake didn't mean to startle her, so he nodded politely and picked up his pace through the whitewashed lobby.

Employees whispered and stared as he passed by, though he couldn't blame them for their odd behavior. He was the leper CEO of Wilder Financial, the boss who rarely peeked his head out of his office. He hated this part of the building—the sterile and impersonal nature of it—which was probably why he never entered through the sweeping front doors. He preferred to show up via helicopter from the pad on the roof, then take the stairs down to his upper-level office. It was easier to keep snooping noses out of his private life that way, too. If anyone got too close and found out he was a three-hundred-year-old werewolf, he was done for.

But today was different.

Today he hoped to see the blond vixen who'd stolen his wine and stopped his heart. He searched every passing face for some resemblance to the woman from the cellar, spotted beauties of all shapes and sizes, but none of them compared. None of them held a candle to Emelia Hudson.

Would he see her walking the lower hallways or would he meet her on the top floor near his office? He held his breath, impatiently waiting until the moment when he'd see her in the light of day.

He entered a packed elevator, and although he was sure the employees were all going up, they exited upon his entrance, leaving him staring at his own reflection when the doors hissed shut. His dark eyes appeared more strained than normal—probably from the insufficient two hours of shut-eye he'd gotten last night—and his hair was unusually messy, nearly flopping into his eyes. He scrubbed his hands over his face and tunneled his fingers through his hair.

When he hit the forty-second floor—the penthouse—and the doors yanked back, Drake clenched and unclenched his fists, shook out his arms and exhaled.

This was it. The moment when he would see Emelia again and know if the connection between them was caused by the wine or something…else.

Raul Bloomfield, his Beta wolf, charged around the

corner and welcomed Drake with a stiff handshake.

"Good morning, boss," he said, handing him a note with missed calls on it, listed in order of importance. "I have to say, you threw quite the party last night."

"Thank you, Raul. They say parties can be judged by the mess they leave in the morning. From the looks of my living room, I'd say it was a riot." Drake skimmed the list and shoved it into his front pocket. He had more important matters to attend to at the moment. "Is Emelia Hudson here yet?"

"No sir, I'm afraid she's running late." Raul pressed down the front of a Brioni coat as straight and black as his hair. Even though his eyes were a muted shade of charcoal, they held an intensity that could strike fear in the heart of any one of their packmates. "But I've briefed Ms. Fox on the new state of affairs. She'll run your business aspects, as usual, and Ms. Hudson will be your personal secretary until you feel she is ready to handle other matters of business."

Drake checked his watch as he marched around the corner and down the long hall leading to his office. "I asked you to have her transferred here first thing this morning. It's nearly noon."

Raul Bloomfield had been Drake's Beta wolf for two hundred years. He'd never taken this long to obey an order. Figures he'd stall on the most important order Drake had ever given him: transfer Emelia Hudson to his private office staff ASAP.

"I contacted the temp agency as you requested," Raul said, following on Drake's heels. "I retrieved all of Ms. Hudson's information from the county, and I'm searching the pack's database for more comprehensive records. I had an extra desk moved outside your door, as requested, and she should be here any minute. I'm told she's running late due to a nasty hangover, sir."

Raul's thoughts raced through Drake's head as if they

were his own. The ancient pack-speaking process was common to him—as ordinary as drinking his coffee black and his scotch Blue—but this time, Raul's silent words turned Drake's feet to stone.

Why do I get the feeling she experienced more than a hangover, sir? Luminaries are reported to experience symptoms that resemble drunken stupor when they meet their fated mate.

"Don't even think it, Raul. I wasted two hundred prime years of my life looking for my Luminary. She's not going to appear as Little Red Riding Hood at one of my office parties a century after I've given up searching for her."

"If you say so, sir."

Despite Drake's ramblings, he knew there was something *off* about his reaction to Emelia. The way she'd looked in that silly costume had captured his interest first—the crimson corset hourglassed her figure and flaunted the plumpness of her breasts, making his mouth water and his hands ache to brush over her skin. She was the sexiest woman he'd ever seen, hands down, oozing sex appeal without trying. But it was the sincerity behind her piercing stare that had held Drake prisoner in the cellar. Those midnight-blue eyes had spellbound him, rendering him speechless, pinching his heart in a vise. He'd never experienced anything like it before.

Emelia Hudson.

Could he really have found her? His Luminary? The idea struck him as ridiculous. He was an Alpha, rightful heir to the Seattle wolf pack throne. She was human. She wasn't a born werewolf, and to be turned would mean she wouldn't be strong enough to have children. Or, in the case that she became his mate, Alpha heirs. In three hundred years, he'd never heard of an Alpha finding a human as his Luminary.

Fate was a nasty bitch, with a twisted sense of humor.

After leaving the cellar last night, Drake had retreated to his room. He'd dived into old texts about the reaction an

Alpha werewolf would have upon finding his one and only Luminary—the eternal light in his life, his soul mate. He'd studied the chemical reaction that sparked between fated lovers upon first touch. Everything was spot-on to how he'd felt down in that cellar…with her.

Still, Drake had to meet her again. Just to be certain. He could've mistaken off-the-charts chemistry with the Luminary reaction, couldn't he? Simply meeting in the halls wouldn't be enough to figure it out. He wanted more than a single touch and a few cordial words in passing. There was too much on the line to take the situation lightly. Drake needed to keep Emelia Hudson close until he knew for sure.

As Drake reached his secretary's desk, Trixie Fox stood and handed him a steaming mug of coffee. It was bold and out-of-the-pot hot, nearly scalding his tongue. The pain quieted Raul's thoughts before they could continue further.

"Good morning, Mr. Wilder," Trixie said with a kind smile.

"I hope the new arrangement's all right." Drake pointed to the second desk across from Trixie's—the one he'd brought in especially for Emelia. The mahogany desks faced each other and flanked his door, creating an alleyway to his office. "I'm not sure if Ms. Hudson will pan out as my personal secretary, but I know how overworked you've been lately. I think it might be more accommodating to split the secretary position into admin and personal."

It wasn't a total lie. Trixie worked her ass off for Wilder Financial, and could absolutely use another set of hands to assist with business—only those hands wouldn't be Emelia's. Drake wasn't sure how long it would take to rule out Emelia as his Luminary, but he'd keep her close until he knew undeniably either way. He made a mental note to find Trixie a real assistant as soon as he ruled Emelia out.

"It means so much knowing that you've noticed how hard I've been working." Trixie tucked her tawny-brown hair behind her ears and smiled coyly. "I was starting to think you didn't see me at all."

Under normal circumstances, Drake would've been flattered by Trixie's constant attention. He couldn't deny she was classically beautiful—taller than average with a model-thin build, generous breasts, and legs that wouldn't quit. But there'd never been a spark between them. At least not from Drake's side. In the five years Trixie had worked for the company, Drake had never gotten the urge to take advantage of the long nights they spent working in his office.

Not once.

"I trust you'll be able to instruct Ms. Hudson on how we run things around here?"

Trixie nodded. "I'll have her in top form in no time."

As far as Drake was concerned, Emelia's form was already top-notch. "I'm sure you will."

Striding toward his office, Drake shot a quick glance at the desk that would soon be Emelia's. Flat-screen monitor. Keyboard. Pad of paper. Telephone. She already had the necessities, though she wouldn't be using those things much. As Drake's personal assistant, she'd refill his coffee, run errands, take orders, and handle things Trixie was too busy to handle herself.

He couldn't wait to see Emelia again.

"Mr. Wilder?" Trixie's voice pierced his thoughts.

He turned and stared into questioning hazel eyes. "Yes?"

"Pardon my saying so, but are you sure you want a temp to fill this position? I'm sure we could find a secretary from a lower department who is more qualified."

"I appreciate your concern, Trixie, and perhaps in a day's time we'll get someone from another department. For now, I want Emelia Hudson and no other."

With a wince, Drake entered his office and waited for the door to click shut behind him.

"You want Emelia Hudson and no other?" Raul's voice taunted.

Drake stood in front of his floor-to-ceiling windows, zoned out on the misty cityscape, and scrubbed his head. Had he really just said that? "Damn, that came out wrong."

"No," Raul said, placing his hand on Drake's shoulder. "There's a chance it came out right."

It'd been nothing more than surprise, Drake thought. Emelia had caught him off guard in the wine cellar last night. He hadn't been with a woman in months. He'd been tense and on edge, tired from dealing with bundles of acquisitions in the city. He'd been all business, impersonal and cold, for so long, she'd been a welcome surprise. She'd somehow soothed him.

She couldn't be his Luminary, his one and only destined mate.

God help him if she was.

Chapter Three

Emelia leaned away from her new desk on the top floor of Wilder Financial and stared at her bottle of Dasani as if it could somehow materialize into a bottle of Advil and take her headache away. She couldn't remember much from last night, which was damn odd considering she'd never blacked out from drinking before.

She did remember Drake, though, and how the feel of his lips made her knees wobble like Jell-O. Even her ex-fiancé—whom she downright refused to think about for another second—hadn't excited her the way Drake had, and they'd had some steamy encounters over the course of their rocky relationship.

There was something different about Drake. Something about the way her stomach flipped and her brain seized… Their connection seemed more than physical. Every time the word "kismet" popped into Emelia's head, she dismissed it. Couldn't let thoughts like that run wild—that's how she got in trouble the last time.

After the way things had ended with her fiancé, the last

thing she needed was to hop into another relationship.

Trixie Fox, the secretary who was supposed to help Emelia settle in to her new job, stood on the opposite side of the large desk, wagging her finger from one side to the other. Emelia could barely make out Trixie's words over the pounding in her head—the sound was muffled and jumbled like the droning teacher from the *Peanuts* television shows.

"Your job is to take care of the daily to-do list, whether it says to pick up Mr. Wilder's dry cleaning, shop for stationery, or coordinate the next office party," *whaa-whaa-whaa*, "make sure you have a cup of extra-hot black coffee ready to hand him the moment he arrives," *whappity-whaa-wha-wha*, "answer the phone," *mwa-wha-mwa-wha-aah,* "leave all messages on his desk. That's about it."

Emelia tried to pay attention to every word, but she went rigid at the mention of Mr. Wilder's name. "This is…" She craned her neck around and stared at the tiny gold plate on the door to her right. Engraved on it were two stenciled black words, and one undeniable title: Russell Wilder, CEO. "You've got to be kidding me."

"Nope, not kidding. Didn't they tell you who you'd be working for?"

Groaning, Emelia slammed her face into her hands, then shook her head. Blond chunks of hair dangled over the desk, tickling her arms. She wasn't ready for this. Not today. Today's mission was to locate Drake, and she'd planned on it taking up her entire day. She'd pushed off Mission Interrogate Wilder until tomorrow…

She looked up, feeling more drained than she had in years. "The agency said top floor. If I didn't have the headache from hell, I might've figured."

Trixie spun around her desk and plopped into the leather seat. As her hazel eyes skimmed over the computer screen, her fingers flew over the keyboard. "Don't know what you did to get transferred here, but I've never seen a newbie move up the ranks that quickly. You'll be able to use this on your résumé for years…if he likes you."

Emelia laughed into a snort. "I don't think I'll have to worry about that."

Not after the way she planned to grill him. Had she really been assigned as Mr. Wilder's secretary? Could it have been that easy? After the longest month of her life, slaving away at whatever petty job the Wilder Financial guppies asked her to do, she was finally going to be able to meet Mr. Wilder face-to-face. She was finally going to get some solid answers.

"I hear you moved up from the mail room," Trixie said, wildly scribbling a note. Long, narrow fingers clutched a silver pen, showing off unnaturally square nails gel-shellacked with red, orange, and yellow shades of autumn. "I'm guessing from your headache that you had a good time at the Halloween party last night?"

Emelia's cheeks flushed hot as she remembered the smoldering passion behind Drake's dark eyes. "I did, actually."

"Did you catch a glimpse of Mr. Wilder?"

"No, wish I had."

She'd planned to seduce Mr. Wilder last night, but it was only to get him into a vulnerable position so he would have to hear her out. He hadn't shown up at the party, which was for the better, as long as she could hunt down Drake in Mr. Wilder's labyrinth of a building. Maybe they could find a janitor's closet and pretend it was a wine cellar. Seeking out a relationship was seriously off Emelia's radar, but playing Five Minutes in Heaven with Drake? Sounded like a perfect way to turn Monday into Funday.

"Well, you'll meet him today, for sure. As soon as he's out of his meeting with Mr. Bloomfield, he'll want to meet you. He always makes a point to personally meet every person on his staff."

Moment of truth.

Emelia swallowed hard as her insides squirmed. What was she so nervous about? This was what she wanted, wasn't it? To meet him and get an apology for illegally buying her bar, then refusing her the common decency of a meeting to straighten things out. Okay, so she wanted to see him suffer, just a little...but it was only to match what he'd put her through the last couple months.

"Peeeerrrfect timing." Trixie's sarcasm rang clear. She leaned back, throwing her arms behind her head. "I forgot to drop off the deposit slips at the bank." She tapped her nails on the desk. Then eyed Emelia curiously. "I need you to hold down the fort for thirty minutes or so. Can you do that?"

"I don't think that's such a good idea. I mean, I've been here a whopping two seconds." An idea struck, as sharp and true as a lightning bolt. She could use the time alone to dig around through some of Mr. Wilder's paperwork. "You know what, on second thought, I'll be fine. What do you need?"

Trixie stood, snatched a few manila folders off her desk along with an overflowing desk basket, and plopped them in front of Emelia. "The documents in the tan folders need to be filed. The cabinet is over there." She pointed to a tall filing monstrosity behind her desk. "The papers in the basket need to be shredded." She slid over a waste bin with a shredder anchored over the top. "Pretty simple. Answer the phone, file, shred, got it?"

Nodding, Emelia got to work, opening all the cabinet drawers behind Trixie's desk to orient herself with where things needed to be. Trixie left quietly, gathering her phone, purse, water, and bank deposit bag before heading to the elevators.

Once Emelia was alone, she grinned slyly and scanned the long, taupe hall that stretched to the opposite end of the building. While the lower floors were whitewashed and sterile, looking more like a doctor's office than a financial building, the upper floor was warm and cozy, reminding Emelia of the insides of a posh cabin...if cabin decorators had elegant taste and more money than Oprah. The halls were empty except for a few small trees that looked like mini-pines and pictures of mountain landscapes.

It was quiet and probably wouldn't stay that way. There was no time to lose.

Emelia sauntered back to her desk, determined not to look like she was in too much of a hurry, and flipped through papers in the shred basket. Nothing but duplicates of receipts, board minutes, and miscellaneous memos. She took out a handful, tapped them into a neat pile, then fed them into the shredder. Low, droning noises escaped down the hall as the papers disappeared into the waste bin. Emelia leaned forward, checking near the elevators for any sign of a party crasher. Coast clear. She fingered through the manila "to file" folder and removed a random piece of paper.

It looked like loan-approval paperwork for a newly acquired building south of Capitol Hill.

"Hmm," Emelia scanned the document quickly. "Looks really important. Bet he'd be pissed if someone messed with his business stuff."

She knew too well what happened when people screwed with other people's livelihoods, then acted like they didn't give a damn.

Maybe she could give Mr. Wilder a taste of his own medicine...

She guided the document into the shredder, relishing the mechanical murmur that followed. The crunch-munch-buzz whispered "*Mr. Wilder's downfall*" into Emelia's ears.

With a pang of guilt that she shrugged off, Emelia ripped another document from its manila bed—"Wilder Financial Acquisitions Report for May 2012." As the machine minced the report, Emelia plucked another "important" document from the folder. And then another. She dove headfirst into shredder heaven.

Within minutes, the folders were thinner than before, and Emelia's shoulders significantly lighter. She'd shredded enough documents to drive someone crazy looking for them when they came up missing. She only hoped that someone was Mr. Wilder.

"At least there'll be more room in the file drawers." Smiling ear to ear, Emelia rolled back from the desk and slid the waste bin farther beneath it. She checked the time on her iPhone. "Trixie didn't mention when we break for lunch. I think it's about time."

"I don't think so," a gravelly voice said from behind her. "Not yet."

Mr. Wilder's office consumed the entire upper floor. There was only one person who could be standing behind her.

Shitdamnshit.

She'd moved too fast, had gotten too close to the fire and had been burned. How much had he seen? Wincing, Emelia spun around.

"Drake?" She blanched.

"Good afternoon, Emelia."

He was just as she remembered through her drunken fog. His shoulders were impossibly broad, his lips curving seductively into a smile. The width of his stance was commanding and stern, matching the hard clench of his jaw. His eyes were dark and brooding, hiding delicious secrets. Her body's reaction to Drake hadn't changed much in twelve hours. Her core heated and shook, quivering with anticipation.

How fast could they get to the nearest closet?

"Wha—what are you doing here?" She searched around his shoulder for Mr. Wilder, peering into the depths of the heartless CEO's office. A stocky man with dark hair and darker eyes stepped out. The perfectly pressed suit he wore probably cost more than a year of her rent. "Mr. Wilder, I presume?"

"Oh, no, but don't I wish." The man laughed, two deep belts that seemed to erupt from his belly. His gaze flipped from Emelia to Drake. "I think my guess was right on the mark, sir. You watch. She's going to be your best personal secretary yet."

A low rumble filled the space between them. Emelia could've sworn it was a growl. Where'd that come from? She double-checked the power light on the shredder.

"That'll be all, Mr. Bloomfield," Drake ordered, then met Emelia's eyes. "Would you mind stepping into my office?"

No, no, no, he had to be kidding; the hard-pressed line of his lips proved otherwise.

"You're not…I mean, you weren't…" As reality hit, Emelia backed against the desk so the urge to jab him in the throat wouldn't overtake her. "You lied to me."

"Well, that depends on how you look at it. Would you mind?" He spread his arm toward his open office door. "I promise I'll only take a few minutes of your time."

The hard glare in Drake's eyes defeated her rejection before she gave it. He wasn't asking for a few minutes with her, alone in his office. He was demanding it. Emelia got the feeling he wasn't turned down often.

"Is your name even Drake?" she snapped, passing through the door.

"My formal, given name is Russell Drake Wilder. I'm named after my father, but as I told you last night, my friends call me Drake."

Damn it. *Russell D. Wilder*. His name was emblazoned over the top of every piece of correspondence that left the building. Okay, so he hadn't lied, but he hadn't exactly been forthcoming with the truth, which was the same in her book.

The door clicked shut and Emelia became hyperaware that very few people were ever invited into his personal space. Not only did he own the elaborate furnishings, he owned the building. Hell, he owned the entire block and the one across the street. He controlled every last ounce of breathable air and everything within the four mocha-painted walls. In this space—*his space*—did he think he ruled over her, too?

Probably. *Ass.*

She stood like a statue in the center of his office, on the edge of a bearskin rug, surrounded by dark leather and well-oiled wood. The place threw off a warm, soothing vibe, yet all Emelia could think about was how numb her insides felt—it was the cold, harsh sting of betrayal.

"You could've said that we were in your cellar, drinking your wine. You could've said your name was Russell. You lied to me." Anger surged through Emelia's veins. First, Drake had tried to rip her bar from underneath her—the only thing she had in the world—and then he'd kissed her, turned her on, and left her in the basement of *his* mansion. He'd lied. Made her feel something for him that wasn't real. Jacking with her business was heartless, but messing with her emotions was on another whole level of snake. "That was really messed up, even for someone like you."

"What's that supposed to mean?" He leaned against his desk, folded his arms and crossed his ankles. He exuded dominance, raw and unyielding. "Someone like me?"

Oh boy. She teetered between telling him what she really thought of him and playing the part of a good little secretary so she could sharpen the dagger she held behind his back.

Decisions, decisions.

Why did he have to look so polished in that suit? The stark contrast between the baby-blue hue of his shirt and the fire in his dark eyes was startling. His good looks were more than distracting—they hindered her thought process completely. Is that how he got away with screwing people out of their livelihoods?

Damn if she'd let him screw with her emotions, too. She pulled a rein on her rapidly firing libido and cinched it around her desire for vengeance.

"I mean that you're a savvy businessman. You play with numbers, figures, and loans all day. You play the stock market, and investors of foreign trade, but playing with someone's emotions? That's just plain evil."

His face didn't twitch, flinch, flex. Nothing. He barely responded to her presence at all. Like the kiss last night never happened.

She shouldn't be feeling like this. He was a serpent in Italian threads. A corporate drone, stuck in the business of trampling kind, hardworking people to advance his own profits. Didn't he care to talk about what happened with the building he'd presumably acquired? Didn't he care to discuss how it was possible that she held a deed to the same building?

"You didn't think I was evil last night," Drake said plainly. "Yet the moment you find out who I am, you have no problem insulting me. I'm sorry about lying to you last night, but I thought you'd act differently if I told you who I really was."

"Damn Skippy."

"Is that a yes?"

She groaned. Was lack of humor a requisite on the Wilder Financial application? "If I'd known you were my boss, I would've been a completely different person. I wouldn't have finished off that bottle of wine, I wouldn't have let myself get so tipsy, and I sure as hell wouldn't have kissed you."

His brow furrowed as he seemed to toss over her words. "Tell me, if you think I'm so evil and hate my name so much, why are you working in a building with my name on it?"

This was it. The moment she'd been waiting for.

Emelia wanted him to hear her out as she told him about

how she'd bought the Knight Owl from her neighbor eight years ago. She wanted to tell him to stick his "legal" plot map in his pipe and smoke it. She'd given years of her life maintaining the Knight Owl and had struggled to keep the bar true to its historically famous roots. She wasn't about to give it up to Wilder Financial so they could demolish the building and turn it into another stale coffee joint.

But as Emelia stared into Drake's warm, mocha-toned eyes, she caught sight of the man from last night. The man who showed her that passion wasn't something that developed over time, or something you had to work at to achieve. True, skin-searing passion was something you either had, or you didn't.

With Drake, she had it.

"Things are changing in my bar, and I'm struggling to catch up," she said, offering a smidgeon of truth. "Profits are low, expenses are high, and I needed other income. My temp company placed me here."

"But you've hated working here so far?"

Emelia nodded slowly.

"I see."

Maybe if she worked as Mr. Wilder's secretary for a week, they would build a mutual respect. When he realized there were hearts behind the businesses he was shutting down, maybe he would be more inclined to listen and understand what she'd been saying all along.

She'd purchased the Knight Owl free and clear.

It wasn't her fault that her neighbor took off with the money and then claimed to have sold the entire building to Wilder Financial. The least Mr. Wilder could do was look over her documents and let her keep the bar that was rightly hers to begin with. She didn't know how much he paid for the building, or how he'd get his money back, but it would have to play out that way, wouldn't it?

Drake took a long sip of his coffee, set down the glossed mug, and stared out onto Seattle's cityscape. Rain misted over the windows, blocking out any particular shapes of buildings in the distance. The entire city was one big blur.

"And I'm an evil businessman." Drake's voice was hoarse. Barley a whisper. "Isn't that what you called me?"

When their eyes met, Emelia caught a glimpse of what looked like pain. Remorse? Sadness? Damn it, there went the pang in her stomach.

"I didn't say *you* were evil. Not exactly. I said *lying* to me was evil."

"I don't think this should be drawn out any longer." He stood, reaching out his hand.

She felt her face puzzle. "What shouldn't be drawn out?"

"Good day, Ms. Hudson."

Emelia eyed Drake's hand carefully, staving off the feeling that she was being baited for something. Shaking his hand was simple, a temporary peace offering. But touching him could unleash the same feelings as last night—she couldn't walk straight for two hours after his lips had touched hers.

"Good day." She curled her fingers around his hand. The instant they touched, electric currents of something hot and palpable sparked over her skin, jump-starting her heart. She jerked back. "Whoa. Must be static electricity."

"Yeah." His eyes shadowed over and he rubbed his hand. "Must be."

Chapter Four

It'd been five days since Drake touched Emelia skin to skin, palm to palm. Five days since he realized that she was, unequivocally, his Luminary. He'd wrapped up business and bailed, taken his helicopter to the airport and flown straight to his home in LA. He had to put space between them so he could think properly.

Two hundred years ago—hell, even last century—Drake would've howled all hours of the day and night to find his Luminary.

His father, Alpha to their pack, had owned and maintained unbelievable amounts of property before he died. Half of Queens and Brooklyn, most of Chicago and Seattle, and decent parts of Los Angeles were all Wilder property. Beyond the property and investments, he ruled over the most powerful werewolf pack in the world.

Handing control to an Alpha heir should've been simple. But Drake had a twin brother, Silas, and it'd been made perfectly clear that sharing control over the pack was not an option.

Knowing the pack wouldn't take commands from two Alphas, Drake's father had decreed that the first son to find his Luminary would become Alpha. The order had been simple. Find your soul mate and control the pack. The other brother would inherit their father's property and be financially set for life. The order had started a nasty race to search out their Luminaries. Silas had been born minutes before Drake and felt that control over the pack should've been given directly to him.

Not wanting to destroy their relationship, Drake told Silas he didn't care to find his Luminary—he'd given up the search. He wouldn't let his thirst for control tear apart their family any longer. He and Silas had found peace, shared profits, worked alongside each other the way they should've all along. Some members of the pack naturally gravitated toward one of them or the other, and there was a large group of army-like mercenaries who refused to declare loyalty until a true Alpha was determined, but for the most part, they'd ruled equally.

But now, finding Emelia—a human, above all else—changed everything.

Silas would sense that Drake had found his Luminary. And he'd know that Drake would take control over the pack he longed to rule alone. That realization wasn't going to sit well with a control freak like Silas.

Drake had planned on staying away from Emelia longer—a month might've weakened the pull between them and fuzzed the signal between Drake and his brother—but he'd gotten sick. Headaches and chills wouldn't quit. Vomiting increased as the days crept on. He hadn't slept a wink.

He'd instructed Raul to dive into ancient werewolf texts to see if there was some mention of the physical or psychological reaction an Alpha would have upon finding his Luminary. Within hours Raul had unearthed something disturbing: once an Alpha and his Luminary touched, they were connected by spirit. Sickness was common during long periods of absence, especially for the male.

Bloody wonderful. Drake was connected to a woman who seemed to hate him, yet if he stayed away from her longer than a few days, he'd be sick. Emelia didn't exactly say she hated him, but Drake sensed unbridled disdain bubbling within her.

As he parked his BMW Roadster in front of the Knight Owl, he leaned beneath the doorframe and stared at the sidewalk welcome sign and warm, glowing interior. Chills gathered at the base of his spine. Why did he feel like he knew the building? He'd never been here before. Never even heard of the place.

The Knight Owl. He would've remembered such a name, wouldn't he?

He exited the car and zipped up his coat, steeling himself against the crisp night wind. As he stepped onto the curb, Drake made a quick call to Raul that went straight to voice mail.

"Find everything you can on the bar called the Knight Owl, located at 970 East Porter Street." He ended the call, hesitating a beat before striding through the front door.

Though the concept was ludicrous, Drake felt better already, merely being near the place that held such a strong tie to Emelia. Strength returned to his legs and the tomato soup he'd forced down at dinner finally settled in his stomach.

Emelia was nearby.

Striding through the creaky door, Drake was slammed with the mouthwatering aroma of BBQ burgers and roasted garlic. The walls were painted rich shades of brown and burgundy. Candles on the tables and lanterns in the corners cast a warm, buttery glow over the room. Mismatched chairs and wood-topped tables could've easily accommodated fifty people, though tonight the space was nearly empty. A group of four college-aged kids fought over a heaping plate of something brown that was situated in the center of their table—garlic-roasted onion strips, from the pungent smell of them. A lone guitarist in desperate need of a shave strummed away on the stage in the corner, giving a horrible rendition of "Stairway to Heaven."

The place had an interesting feel. It had character. Spice. And it was so unlike the other bars he'd visited in Seattle.

Newspaper clippings in gold-tinseled frames covered the walls, snagging Drake's attention. As an older couple emerged from the back half of the building and made their way toward the exit, Drake moved aside to let them pass. The faded headline of an article from October 30, 1929, caught his interest.

Dow Plummets Thirty Points. Wall Street Scrambles to Recover.

Drake remembered the day after the stock market crash well. He and Silas fought over whether to pull cash from their investments and hide it in overseas accounts or hold tight and ride out the drought. Seemed like they couldn't agree on anything.

"Hi, handsome. What can I getcha?" The brunette waitress who'd slid up next to Drake reeked of cheap cherry-blossom lotion. Chopped, razor-short hair framed a heart-shaped face and thin lips.

"I'm here to see Emelia." The sledgehammer pounding into Drake's temple eased up at the mention of her name.

"She's working the bar on the flip side. Want me to call her for you?" The waitress smiled politely, the piercings on her upper lip, chin, and eyebrows shining in the flickering overhead lights. Why women thought they had to drive nails of silver into their skin to attract men was beyond him.

"No, I was hoping to surprise her." Drake gave one of his deviously slow winks. "You won't give away my secret, will you?"

"Not at all." She shook her head as the scent of her arousal hit Drake's heightened senses. "If you change your mind, and decide you want something after all...*anything*... let me know. My name's Renee."

"Thanks," Drake said. "I'll remember that."

With one last glance at the deserted front of the bar, Drake stalked around the wall that split the building in half and stopped as his heart gave a jerk.

Emelia stood behind a long, wooden bar, shaking a drink. Flipping the silver can in her palm, she poured the yellowish liquid into a glass and smiled when a tiny red straw dropped and spun, facing the customer in front of her.

Drake's gaze stuck to her like glue. The entire building could've gone up in flames and he would've stayed to watch Emelia a minute longer. Her hips swayed confidently as she walked to the opposite end of the dimly lit room. She smiled at a scruffy-bearded fellow wearing worn flannel and suspenders, laughed when he laughed, and lit up the entire bar. She was personable and friendly, refilling the drink of a curly-haired woman trying to catch the eye of a Goth-dressed guy standing next to her. Even though there were only three customers perched at the watering hole, Emelia spun to the till as if roller skates had replaced her shoes. She was all bar business, decked in ripped jeans and a black, lace-trimmed tank. Sexy as hell.

In her natural space, Emelia didn't fit the secretary bill Drake had initially pinned on her. *Thank God.* He wasn't sure what he expected from Emelia, being a temp and all, but he'd never been hot and heavy over one of the ladies on his staff, and was secretly hoping his Luminary would have a passion for something other than filing papers.

Sliding onto the nearest stool, Drake was amazed Emelia hadn't spotted him yet. On second thought, maybe she had and was choosing to ignore him. The thought made something in Drake's chest pinch. Rubbing the spot with his hand, Drake watched as Emelia placed an order through the window on the far side of the bar. An older man with short, spiky hair peeked his face through the window and held his gaze on Emelia's backside a little too long for Drake's taste.

"What does a guy have to do to get a drink around here?" Drake said a little too loudly, leaning into an umbrella of amber light.

Emelia spun around slowly, as though she'd sink into quicksand if she moved too fast. With a nervous smile pulling at her lips, she approached him, tossing a napkin on the bar.

"We don't have Lafite," she said, wiping her hands on her jeans, "or anything like what you've got in that cellar of yours."

"Do you have scotch?" He removed his coat, draped it over the stool next to him, and tipped his chin at the top glass shelf.

She pulled down a bottle of Johnnie Walker Blue Label, Drake's favorite and the most expensive in the brand, and poured a stout glass. "Ice?"

"Straight."

"You sure you don't want to hit the BevMo across town? You could save yourself the thirty-five-dollar shot and invest in the bottle." She slid the glass across the bar; it stopped right on the mark, right in front of him. "Not that I couldn't use the money."

Drake held up the glass in mock cheers and took a sip. The smoky drink warmed his insides and erased the last hint of sickness that'd plagued him over the week.

Who was he fooling? The ease of tension in his middle had nothing to do with the scotch.

Moving with a kind of grace Drake hadn't seen often, Emelia checked on Mr. Lumberjack at the end of the bar and refilled his beer. She wiped up a mess Mr. Goth had just made and double-checked to make sure Ms. Corkscrew didn't want to order another round. When Emelia circled back around to Drake, she stared as if she expected him to poof into a cloud of smoke and disappear once more. That wasn't happening. Not now. Not when he had the chance—away from prying company eyes—to get to know his Luminary.

"So this is your place?" Drake had been curious about the Knight Owl. He hadn't expected a newspaper-clad bar with a dark, tavern feel. The bar wasn't the kind of place he'd normally visit. It was warm and friendly and gave an unconventional, homey vibe. "It's clever."

"What are you doing here, Mr. Wilder?" Emelia's hands found her hips, but attitude didn't follow. She looked nervous. Like he'd invaded her turf and caught her being nice when it was the last thing she wanted. "Don't tell me you came to pay compliments to my bar. I might have to hurl."

Drake's stomach wrenched. "For the love of God, don't mention hurling."

"Mr. Wilder, are you all right? You look…green." She eyed him carefully. "Like Kermit green, you know? The men's room is right over there."

She hitched her thumb like a hiker, pointing over her shoulder to the main room, but Drake's gaze didn't follow. He focused on breathing. In and out, in and out. He closed his eyes. Despite the overwhelming aroma of his scotch, Emelia's natural feminine scent invaded his nose. As tantalizing hints of warm sugar, and something a bit sweeter, worked their way through Drake's senses, coating away the last of the queasiness, he sighed. Emelia truly was the calm to his storm, the *Chicken Soup* to his howling soul.

And he was royally botching this.

"You've been MIA all week," she said, her voice like liquid velvet.

Drake opened his eyes and drank in the softness of Emelia's features: gently rounded chin, high cheekbones, silky, honey-blond hair flowing to her shoulders. She was a goddess. Aphrodite in human form.

And she'd noticed his absence.

Before Drake got too excited, a hard bout of logic sucker-punched him in the gut. Of course Emelia noticed. She sat in front of his office door all damned day. *Idiot.*

"Glad to hear that I've been missed," he teased. He could've sworn Emelia shuddered before averting her eyes.

"Wouldn't count on it." She snatched a wet glass off the drying rack and toweled the rim, scraping it like she aimed to shave it down to sand.

"Has Mr. Bloomfield been showing you the ropes well enough?"

"Not as good as you." Her eyes widened as if she caught herself. "What I mean is, there were some things I wanted to talk to you about this week…" She paused, her gaze snapping to the kitchen as a plate banged against a sink. "Where've you been, anyway?"

"I had business to take care of in LA." He drank to soothe the burn in his throat. "I won't be going back there for a long while now."

Not unless he wanted to compete in the Influenza Olympics. There was no way his businesses could slow down, no way he could ignore the work that had to be done at his offices around the country.

Emelia would just have to come with him, though he wasn't sure how he felt about it yet. She was easy on the eyes—understatement of the year—but she also had a mouth like a sailor and Drake never knew what she was going to say, or do, next. Wild cards never panned out well. Not in a business run by logistics and numbers and margin calls. Drake had built his life around predictability, only inviting people he could trust into his inner circle.

Mother Nature certainly had a twisted sense of humor, matching him with a loose-cannon bartender…a *human*, loose-cannon bartender, no less.

"So you come back into town and decide to stop by my bar?" she asked, eyebrows pitching. "No offense, but you don't look like my typical customer. Most of my patrons can't afford the tie cinched around your neck."

"This one?" Drake eyed his charcoal-gray, Italian silk tie lying against his pristinely white Forzieri dress shirt. The ensemble had been purchased by his stylist—she'd said it exuded powerful grace. He thought she was full of shit, but the clothes fit well, so he couldn't complain. "This tie couldn't have cost more than fifty."

More like three hundred, but who cared?

"Is that so?" she said, a playful gleam in her eye.

Leaning over so that the swell of her breasts pressed against the bar, Emelia dragged a finger across Drake's chest. He fought to keep his eyes off the plumpness of her breasts as his slacks tightened at the seams. She smiled, slow and teasing, as she spun small circles over his pectoral muscles. Drake's mouth dried as blood froze in his veins. He couldn't get their kiss out of his head, couldn't forget the way her lips had felt brushing against his. She was so close. All he'd have to do is lean forward, drag his hands through her hair, and catch her mouth.

They weren't in his building or on duty. They wouldn't be doing anything wrong. He could kiss her, drive her crazy, pleasure her in the back room, and they wouldn't be breaking any company rules. Hell, even if they were, he was the damned boss. If it meant kissing Emelia again, he'd rewrite the whole company-relations book to include a boss-secretary-

Luminary loophole.

Emelia leaned farther forward. Drake's breath sucked in as a hiss. She latched on to the bottom of the tie like it was a rein, gave it a commanding tug, then flicked it, whacking him in the nose. She laughed the way she had in the cellar, carefree and playful, her smile wide and bright like a Colgate ad.

The woman was trying to kill him.

"Very funny," he said, as she went back to drying glasses. How could she be so unaffected by their closeness? "You're right—bars aren't normally my thing. This place has a unique quality about it, I'll give you that. It stands out in this neighborhood like a gem."

Just like its owner.

Something he said pulled down the corners of Emelia's lips. For the first time since he'd seen her in the bar, she went rigid. "Yeah, well, if big businesses keep stepping in and shutting places like this down, there'll be no personality left in Seattle. Everyone will walk around town like corporate drones with Palm Pilot styluses shoved up their asses."

There came the surge of anger again. It flowed off Emelia in tangible waves. How could she be hot one minute, nearly scorching his skin through his clothes, and be as cold as ice the next? Was a big business threatening to shut down her bar? Was that the cause for her hostility? Whatever the reason, Drake had to diffuse the situation, especially if they were going to be attached at the hip for the next couple hundred years.

How would that work, anyway? How could he take control over a pack if he couldn't produce an heir? And would Emelia want to be turned? Would she want to bond with him at all? There were too many questions and not enough blood flowing through his brain to think them all through.

"I think we started off on the wrong foot, Emelia. What do you say we start fresh?"

"Fresh?"

"Let's pretend the wine cellar never happened." *How could he forget?* "I'm not your boss and you're not my secretary. What if I'm just a guy who walked into your bar?"

"You can't hide who you really are." Emelia slid a fifty-cent tip off the bar and dropped the quarters into a mason jar next to the till. "You can staple antlers on a dog, but that won't make him a reindeer."

Laughter erupted from Drake's chest. "You say the craziest shit sometimes, you know that?"

"Haven't you ever seen *How the Grinch Stole Christmas*?"

"Can't say I have."

She tilted her head and shrugged. "Sounds like you had a pretty boring childhood."

Images of intense Alpha training—military-school-esque—in remote portions of the Sierra Nevadas flickered through Drake's brain like an old movie reel. The laughter that had bounced through him moments before flatlined. He took a solid drink, then nodded solemnly. "If you only knew."

"Listen," Emelia said, her voice as soft and smooth as a lover's caress, "the whole 'starting fresh' thing sounds dandy, but you're still Russell Drake Wilder, CEO of a Fortune 500 company, and I'm still Emelia Hudson, your temp secretary. You're not some guy who walked into my bar…you're the guy who thinks he bought it."

"I'm…what? What am I?" Drake slowed down her words. "I think I bought it? I'm pretty sure I would remember having a hand in this place."

She backed against the register as an invisible wall slammed between them, frigid and impassable. "Are you honestly going to sit there and pretend you don't know a thing about what's been happening in your own company?"

Here it was, the reason for the anger. Drake stood, kicked his foot up on the stool, and went palms-down on the bar.

"Give it to me straight, Emelia. What are we talking about here?"

She fidgeted, planting her hands on her hips, crossing her arms over her chest, then shoving her hands into her pockets. Whatever she had to say was tying her in knots. The desire to stroke his hand down her cheek and tell her that it would be all right nearly overcame him. But he didn't know what the real problem was, he reminded himself. How could he promise that things would be all right when he truly didn't know what was bothering her?

Her words had to be off the mark; Drake would've remembered taking out a loan for new property. "What is it you think I did to you and your bar?"

Emelia's eyes weighed heavy with burden as she opened her mouth to speak, then clamped it shut again. The longer the silence stretched between them, the more strain showed in the tightness of her lips.

Damn, Drake hated seeing her this way. He preferred the fun-loving Little Red he met in the cellar, when she didn't care about being seen as ridiculous and foolish. There weren't many people like that in his life—people who made him laugh from his belly and forget that he had a job to do and a business to run. He enjoyed seeing Emelia's inner light shine when she bartended, when she didn't know he was watching. He hated the fact that something he did made her guarded and fidgety, questioning her thoughts before they formed into words.

The bell from the kitchen dinged loudly, severing their connection. It dinged again, and again, two loud chirps that came from an irritated hand.

"Order up," the cook hollered, staring through the kitchen's window. "Emelia, this one's yours for the group out front."

"Have Renee take it out."

"She's on break."

Sighing heavily, Emelia shook her head and seemed to snap back to business mode. The curtain behind her eyes returned, blocking the anger from taking front and center stage.

"I shouldn't have opened that can of worms, not here," Emelia said, swiping two full trays off the kitchen sill. "You took me off guard, showing up mid-shift like this. Can we talk later? Tomorrow morning, maybe? In your office?"

"Tomorrow's Saturday."

"You're telling me you don't work weekends?"

"Of course I do, I was thinking about you. Aren't you going to want to sleep in tomorrow?"

Isn't that what normal people did? Work nine to five, then relax with family, friends, and lovers on weekends? As the thought struck him, Drake realized he hadn't checked Emelia's personal background. He hadn't seen a ring, thank the stars above, but that didn't mean there wasn't a constant "someone" in her life.

"Don't worry about me," she said. "I can take care of myself."

"It's a man's job to take care of his woman." The words tumbled out as Drake's head went light. His mating instincts sure took the wrong moment to flare up. Time to get fresh air before he started humping her leg. Drake peeled a fifty out of his money clip and dropped it on the bar, then draped his coat over his arm.

As Emelia's eyes narrowed to slits and she opened her mouth, probably to tell him how she wasn't his woman, Drake said, "What time do you close tonight? It'd be my pleasure to give you a ride home."

"No, there's no need for that, I've got my car." Emelia tilted her head to the side. As though she was weighing Drake's offer and intention. "I think it'd be best to talk tomorrow anyway…temptation sleeps better during the day."

What the hell was that supposed to mean? Why couldn't she talk like a normal person so he could understand her? What was with all the damn Skippys, stapling antlers, and sleeping temptation talk?

"You really need to get out of the office a little more often." She blew rogue strands of blond hair out of her face, giving Drake a glimpse of something feral churning in her sapphire eyes. "I meant that I won't be tempted to invite you inside my place for a nightcap if I don't allow you to drive me home."

Emelia disappeared around the corner, handling the trays like a pro.

As Drake finished off the remnants of his drink and left the bar, he couldn't help but smile. No matter how much Emelia wanted to hate him, he'd somehow gotten under her skin.

Chapter Five

Emelia locked up the bar twenty minutes after closing and stepped out onto Porter Street as light plumes of rain drifted down from the sky. She always loved the rain, the way it washed away dirt and grime from the city streets, leaving behind the crisp, curt smell of wet asphalt. Taking a deep breath, she flipped her hood over her head and trudged toward the parking lot across the street.

She fished her keys out of her bag before she approached her green Civic and unlocked it. Years of working in this neighborhood had taught her that one could never be too prepared; she always unlocked her car before she reached it, and she always carried mace. In the month Emelia had worked at Wilder Financial, she'd never had to worry about her safety. Not like this. The place was run like a fort—tight security at the front, mazes of halls to get lost in, and cameras trained on every bustling street corner.

The streets in this part of town were quiet tonight, Emelia realized, scanning one way, then the other. Usually she could hear the hum of the city, the occasional bum collecting bottles out of waste bins. Tonight, there was nothing but the soft pitter-patter of rain against the ground.

And suddenly, footsteps pounding over pavement. Behind her.

Emelia spun, digging a hand into her bag to search out the mace.

Breath froze in her lungs as the biggest, most rugged man she'd ever seen charged across the street and set haunting yellow eyes upon her. His bald head glistened with rain, and the leather coat tightening over his chest shone oil-slick black. He was six-foot-six, three hundred pounds of menacing biker.

Holy Son of Anarchy.

Emelia ran around the back of her car to the driver's-side door, heart pounding double-time. She opened the door and glanced up before sliding inside. Once the biker was over the curb and in the parking lot, he slowed to a stop and threw up his hands. Strange tattoos were etched into his palms, swirling out toward his fingers. He bent low, peering beneath the doorframe from a solid thirty feet away. Fumbling with her keys, Emelia shoved the right one into the ignition…and paused, when he smiled.

"I didn't mean to frighten you," he said, inching closer. "My bike broke down around the corner and my phone's dead." He held up his cell phone, shaking it side to side like a dead mouse strangled in his fat fingers. "Could I use yours?"

Why was she hesitating? Because her green heap of metal had broken down more times than she could count, leaving her stranded in strange places, too? He might be in genuine need of help. It was raining and the streets *were* unusually empty tonight…

She glanced through the window at the hard lines of his face, the severe cut of his jaw, and the sheer size of his hands. If he clenched his fists, they'd be the size of melons! A man like that should've been fully capable of taking care of himself.

She followed her instincts.

"No, sorry!" Emelia yelled through the window, then started the car.

At the sound of the engine sputtering to life, the man sprinted and leaped like a damned gazelle, landing with a deafening thud on the roof of her car.

What the hell?

Screaming, Emelia ducked from the bend and groan of the Civic's roof. She threw the car into reverse. Hit the gas hard and backed over a parking block. The car jolted and rocked, and a deafening growl vibrated the air like thunder.

Thoughts tangled in Emelia's head, sticky and incomprehensible. She had to get out of here. What was happening? What was that noise? Who the hell was that guy and why did he jump on top of her car?

Panic sliced through Emelia like a stinging whip. She slammed the car into drive, lead-footed the gas pedal and cranked the wheel toward Porter Street. She plunged down the lot exit at high speed, ripping off her bumper as the Civic's front end gnawed on the asphalt. A fist from above slammed through her driver's side window. She screamed, cowering against the flying shards of glass. But as her hands covered her face, Emelia lost control of the wheel. She veered hard to the right, headed toward a parked car. The biker's arm snaked through the window and snatched Emelia by the throat. She clutched at his arms and tried to scream again, but the sound escaped as a strangled cry.

Clawing into the biker's skin, Emelia struggled for air. Her lungs tightened, seizing when nothing came down the chute. Emelia pinched her eyes shut and braced for the collision with the parked car. Everything happened so quickly, it was a mangled blur.

They collided with what felt like a brick wall. Emelia's chest slammed against the steering wheel, sending off starbursts of searing pain into her ribs and down her legs. Her head spun and her eyes blurred. The biker's hand was clutched around her throat one second, and the next, his massive body was thrown onto the hood. She could breathe! Hot streams of air filled Emelia's windpipe, burning on the way to her lungs.

Emelia peeled her eyes open. Was that…Drake?

Relief washed over her, and for a split second, Emelia thought he looked more like a knight in shining armor and less like a heartless, calculating jerk.

Drake stood in the center of the road like a steel wall, drenched from head to foot, rain streaming down his scowling face. He glared at the biker, who'd slid off the hood looking unscathed and pissed-off as hell. Why were they standing there like that? Staring at each other, saying nothing, breathing hard, in the middle of the street?

If the biker hadn't been standing so close to her driver's door, Emelia would've bolted. Instead, she ducked below the wheel and watched, rubbing her tender ribs.

The biker mashed his fist against his chin and popped his neck, then jerked back his shoulders and stood tall, towering over Drake. Clenching his fists, preparing for a fight, Drake snarled with a smile. His teeth were ginormous, blindingly white, and more jagged than any steak knives Emelia had ever seen.

She had to be seeing things. Drake's teeth almost looked like…well, they almost looked like canine teeth, protruding from his gums into razor-sharp points. The biker laughed and spit in Drake's face, as his back hunched awkwardly and his shoulders broadened. He *grew*.

That couldn't be right.

Swiping condensation off the glass, Emelia leaned forward to get a better look, just as a gunshot rang out from somewhere on the sidewalk. With a guttural moan, the biker fell back and hit the hood, then slid onto the asphalt, clutching at a strange silver vial sticking out of his neck.

But Drake didn't have a gun. Emelia peered through the rain battering the windshield, scanned the sidewalk, and spotted someone else—Mr. Bloomfield?—holding a pistol at arm's length. The burly man holstered the gun in the side of his pants and approached the biker's side. He and Drake exchanged words, though Emelia's ears still rang from the shot.

This couldn't be happening. Emelia was dreaming. She was in her apartment, warm in bed, having a nightmare. That was it. Had to be. Things like this didn't happen. In movies like *The Avengers*, maybe, but not in real life. Feeling woozy, Emelia placed a hand on her heart—it raced like a rabbit's, thumping wildly against her hand. Her chest was tight, her breathing shallow. She was going to hyperventilate if she didn't calm down, but how could she after what just happened?

Drake was beside her in a flash, kneeling outside the driver's door. When had she opened it?

"Are you all right?" He put a chilly, wet hand to her forehead. "You feel cold."

"Of course I'm cold, I've been in the rain."

"Oh, good," he said, as his shoulders lost their tension. "If you're well enough to have an attitude, you're going to be fine."

Emelia laid her head back on the headrest and tried to calm herself. Blood rushed through her veins; her heart thumped in her ears. That biker dude was probably dead in the middle of the street and Drake was…what? A hero? An accomplice to murder? "What happened to him? To the biker dude?" Pointing, Emelia tried to rise up, but Drake held her against the seat.

"Everything's going to be okay, I promise. Just leave it to me," he said, though she didn't believe him. No way. Didn't he witness what just happened? "Mr. Bloomfield is taking care of everything now. There's nothing to worry about."

"Nothing to worry about?" she screeched. "Are you insane?"

"I just need to get out of here before the cops show up, and then I'll explain." His words came out flat and emotionless, like he'd dodged the cops a thousand times before. He slid an arm beneath Emelia's legs, swiveling her body so that her feet touched the ground. Her skin tingled beneath her soaked jeans. "Come on, let me give you a ride home."

"But my car...I can't just leave it here." Her world swirled, in and out, in and out, fuzzing when she focused on slowing things down. "And why would we run from the cops? We didn't do anything wrong. That guy tried to kill me. You and Mr. Bloomfield saw it...didn't you?" She braced the steering wheel. "God, I'm so dizzy. I think I'm going to pass out."

"You're having a panic attack. You need to close your eyes and calm down." His fingers curled possessively around Emelia's arm. As though he'd toss her over his shoulder and carry her out of the car if she refused to leave. "I'll take care of everything, but I need you to trust me."

A dark, shadowed figure appeared at Drake's side, tapped him on the shoulder, and handed him something. Yup, that was Mr. Bloomfield all right. Short, stocky, and stinking of Old Spice.

"I don't, Drake. I don't trust you at all." Emelia closed her eyes anyway as something bit her backside, just below her hip. Her skin warmed, burning where she'd felt the sting. "Oww! That burns! Was that a wasp?"

"Sleep, Emelia." Tender fingers, much too tender to be Drake's, brushed sopping tendrils of hair out of her face. "We'll work on the trust when you wake up."

...

"She's going to hate me for drugging her." Drake tugged the sheets to cover Emelia's exposed shoulder. "And she'll have every right."

"You could've let her see the cleanup," Raul said. "It took two seconds to drag him to the trunk of the limo, and Ms. Hudson wouldn't have gotten close enough to the body to see anything anyway."

"He'd already begun the transformation when you tranquilized him, and Emelia's much too observant." Drake lowered his voice so he wouldn't wake her. "She would've asked questions I'm not willing to answer. There was no other choice."

"Then I'm glad I brought extra tranquilizer darts with me. I must admit, sir," Raul said, "I've never seen you hold off the change as well as you did. I expected you to shift long before I got the tranquilizer loaded up."

"I couldn't let her see me that way."

They weren't exactly on the best of terms, but any chance Drake had of getting close to Emelia would've evaporated the instant he shifted into wolf form.

As it was, they'd cut it close. He wasn't sure how much Emelia had seen, but he'd soon find out. She'd have a million questions, and he'd have to come up with answers that were as close to the truth as possible. If there was any chance of them being together, he had to reveal the truth to her slowly, and when she was ready.

"Why the hell was there a werewolf on that street? Emelia's probably gone her whole life without running into a single one of us. She meets me and gets attacked. There's no way that's a coincidence." Drake scrubbed his hands over his face. "I shouldn't have left her alone in that bar."

"You went back, sir." Raul brought over a glass of water and set it on the bedside table. "There are too many members of our pack for you to monitor the second one goes rogue."

"You really think he was from our pack?"

"What are you implying, sir?"

Drake shook his head. "I'm not implying anything. It's just too bad he died before giving up any information."

"Perhaps next time I'll nail him with one dart, sir, instead of six."

Drake bit back a laugh. "One can never be too careful."

Emelia stirred. Little mewing sounds escaped her lips as she rolled over and clutched the sheet against her chest. Something stirred in Drake's rib cage and he dragged his gaze away. She was innocent, oblivious to what she'd gotten herself into. It was staggering how quickly her reality was going to change when she was ready to accept it.

He hadn't known Emelia long, but he knew she was full of life with a bright, bubbly spirit. She didn't ask to be tugged down into their twisted pack dynamic. She wasn't born a werewolf like the others in his pack—how could she be expected to understand a world filled with werewolves and Luminaries and pack mentalities?

Sighing, Emelia rolled over to face Drake, and tossed the sheets off her body like it was a sweltering summer night. She threw her arms over her head and moaned, robbing the moisture from Drake's lips. Her tank top had drifted up, revealing a flat stomach and a sexy little belly button... with a silver ring hooked through it. Drake's breath caught in his throat at the sight. He took back every nasty thought he'd ever had about piercings being trashy or unnecessary or frivolous. All he could think about was smudging kisses over her stomach and gently raking that ring through his teeth.

"Raul, I want you to check into movements of Silas's European group." Drake steeled himself for the words. "They've remained small and mobile, but I think we have some guys who can track them. I hate to think Silas would stoop this low and try to kill Emelia before we complete the bond, but I'd be stupid not to look into it."

"Will do, sir." He let himself out without a sound.

Drake leaned forward, his gaze skimming over Emelia's succulently rounded breasts, the long, slender curve of her neck, and her petal-pink lips. Her skin was remarkably pale against his black satin sheets. She looked like a porcelain doll with a wild mane of blond hair.

He didn't want to think Silas's yearn for total dominance would cause him to send out a hit on an innocent woman, but he couldn't ignore the humming in his gut, either.

Something wasn't right.

Chapter Six

Emelia smelled the doughnuts before she saw them. Her stomach rumbled, and for a split second she'd forgotten everything: the biker, the attack, Drake.

She gasped, shooting out of bed. Good Lord, it wasn't even her bed. It was a steel-poster king-size bed built for a mammoth. The black-cherry covers had been folded back and the satin sheets had been pulled up. Someone had covered her.

Instinctively, Emelia clutched at her chest. Beneath her hands, her ribs were sore and tender to the touch, but a tank top covered her breasts and pants covered her bottom. She was still dressed.

Thank God.

Where the hell was she? The room was cloaked in shadow, with heavy drapes covering the entire wall on the left side of the room. A flat-screen television—had to be at least a 90-inch, the biggest she'd ever seen outside of a theater—was mounted on the wall in front of her, and below that was a small table filled with breakfast goodies.

Towers of pancakes, an opened box of doughnuts, plates full of bacon and sausage, and—heavenly Keurig above—coffee ripped Emelia out of bed. She scrambled to the table, shoved the first cup she spotted under the Keurig machine and punched *brew*. The lapping sound of coffee hitting porcelain made her stomach clench into a hard fist.

How long had it been since she'd eaten? She was starving…and determined to mow down the entire breakfast spread before someone opened the door and caught her. She shoved a doughnut into her mouth, chomped away, and chased it with a taste of coffee. If she was going to get out of here, wherever "here" was, she would need her strength. Yup, that was it: doughnuts plus coffee equaled strength. She'd always been killer at math.

She groaned, savoring the sticky glaze of the doughnut, as someone knocked on the door. Nearly choking down the food, Emelia frantically searched for a way out. Windows? Bathroom? Could she fit under the bed?

"Emelia, you awake?"

Drake.

"Mmeah," she fumbled with a mouthful. "But donncomein, I'mmnotdecent."

The knob turned anyway. Damn it. Emelia dropped the mangled doughnut on the table, set down the coffee, and wiped her mouth with sticky fingers.

Drake strode inside the room and flicked on the light, stopping when their eyes met. Emelia felt like a deer in headlights, frozen when every instinct in her body should've been screaming at her to scramble out of there. He wore dark dress pants slung low on his hips and a steel-gray dress shirt rolled up at the sleeves and unbuttoned to mid-chest. Ripples of tan muscle bulged beneath the shirt, leading to biceps that might've been bigger than her thighs. He seemed to flex and tighten under the weight of her stare.

The sheer size of him, and the way he stood so stoically as if he didn't know what to say, brought memories of the night in front of the Knight Owl raining down.

"What happened?" Emelia fired. "Where am I?"

"You're at my place. I hope you slept all right." He paused, staring at her face, her lips, then reached out for her mouth. "You've got—"

She flinched, not trusting a single move he made. "What are you doing?"

"You're..." His eyes squinted to dark and stormy slits. Drake swiped his tongue over his bottom lip and reached out hesitantly. "You've got something..."

"What?" She backed away, rubbing her bottom lip, her cheek. "Spit it out."

His stony demeanor cracked as a smile curved his lips. "You've got a glaze mustache."

Disaster. Drake was drop-dead gorgeous, and wore business attire in his own damn home. Emelia was a doughnut-slathered, hyperventilation-prone bartender, wearing the same clothes from last night. They were in two completely different leagues. The unevenness of their pedestals had never been clearer.

Wait, she scoffed to herself, who cared if Drake was once nominated as *Forbes* Businessman of the Year? He'd shot down the biker on the street like it was nothing!

Emelia smothered her lips with a napkin. "Better?"

Drake nodded, shoved his hands into his pockets, and took a giant step back. "I didn't mean to disturb your breakfast. I thought I heard stirring up here and came to take a look."

She swiped her hands on her jeans and licked the last traces of sugar from her lips. Drake's eyes seemed to darken, shadowing from brown to matte black.

"I'm done eating anyway," Emelia said curtly, humiliated that she'd slept in Drake's bed and eaten his food. She should be at her place, in her own bed, rummaging through her fridge for something that wasn't stale. "What am I doing here?"

"Saturday night, after I left your bar, I came home and did some work, then decided that I wanted to see you home after all." He brewed a cup of coffee for himself and settled into the plush leather chair in the corner. "Mr. Bloomfield drove me back, and I did business in the backseat until you closed for the night. I got so absorbed in the stock roll that I didn't see you lock up. I didn't know what was happening until you came barreling out of the parking lot."

"What...*did* happen?" She needed to hear the words from his lips before she went ape-shit.

He tapped the edge of his mug. "What do *you* think happened?"

"Some of the details are a bit fuzzy, but I remember some biker dude wanted to use my phone, and I remember seeing him leap on top of my car." She shuddered at the creepy mental image. As she tried to sift through the haze of the rest of the night, Emelia mindlessly picked up another doughnut and settled on the edge of the bed. Her side ached, just below her hip. She rubbed the spot, then met Drake's guilt-ridden gaze. "Something bit me right before I zonked out."

"I should explain." He took a deep, labored breath. "I used a very mild tranquilizer dart to put you to sleep."

"You...*what*?"

"You were panicking when I needed you to stay calm. I had to get out of there quickly and knew you'd ask a ton of questions and slow our escape."

"So you *drugged* me?" As white-hot pulses of anger surged through Emelia's veins, she chucked the doughnut at Drake's head. He dodged it effortlessly, causing it to splat against the wall behind him. "Who does that? Are you sick? Do you belong to some Seattle-based mafia?"

"I'm sorry, Emelia." Sucker looked sincere with his plush,

downturned lips. "I swear I'll never do anything like that again. I'm not mafia of any kind, and you were never in any danger."

Emelia's insides squirmed—she had to move. She plopped down her coffee cup on the makeshift buffet before striding out of the room. "You didn't roofie the coffee, did you?"

"I'm not a creep," Drake said, following her down the brightly lit hall. "I did what I had to do to protect you and get you out of there. I'm not going to slip something into your drink to have my way with you while you're unconscious."

"Wouldn't put much past you now," she snapped.

Stopping at the top of the stairs, Emelia looked right, down a hallway lined with marble figures. Looked left, down another hallway just as elegant as the other. She'd stepped out of Drake's bedroom and right into the Louvre. She hadn't remembered seeing such elegant masterpieces the night of the office party—he must've had his valuables moved out. Golden blankets of sunshine spilled through the massive skylights, casting favorable light over his entire great room. Artwork in gold-trimmed frames and elaborate tapestries covered the walls while knights in full armor seemed to guard every closed hallway door.

"Do you honestly believe I'm capable of something like that?" Drake followed her winding flight down the stairs, his hand sweeping over the banister moments behind hers. "If you'd slow down a minute we could clear some things up."

Emelia couldn't stop. She had to move so she could think straight. What was she implying, anyway? That Drake slipped something in her coffee so he could have his way with her?

On the outside, Drake masterfully played the part of a lying, shrewd businessman. But Emelia got the feeling that it was a show, a staged front to hide a warm vulnerability beneath the chilly persona. There had to be more to Drake than an expensive suit and a multibillion-dollar business.

No matter how much she disliked his business practices, she knew he wouldn't take advantage of her physically. It was female intuition. A sixth sense. She trusted her gut, which meant she trusted him. On some level.

"No," she said finally. "I don't think you'd stoop that low."

She charged around a marble statue at the foot of the stairs—a woman lying on the ground, with a fanged beast gently cradling her from behind.

Fangs. Last night, hadn't she seen...hadn't Drake's teeth looked...abnormal?

Stopping as if she'd seen a ghost, Emelia spun around and nearly crashed into Drake's chest. His teeth were perfectly straight and brilliantly white. Probably veneers. The shock from the whole incident, mixed with the rain and the panic episode, must've screwed with her vision.

"You can accuse me of being a ruthless businessman, and I might even agree with you on certain occasions," he said.

Finally, an admission of Drake's callous business practices; now they were getting somewhere.

"But I'd never push myself on a woman."

The vein on his neck fluttered madly, capturing Emelia's interest. He seemed so calm and controlled, like a steadily rolling storm, yet his heart was racing. She'd been right in her assessment of him—Drake hid beneath a stoic, controlled image even though passion roiled beneath the surface. Emelia bet that if someone studied Drake long enough, they would get to know all his tells. If he wanted to keep his fortune, Emelia thought, he should stay far away from the poker tables.

"Women deserve to be treasured and treated with respect," he said, as Emelia continued to study the telling vein. She got the feeling he whispered from a dark, secret part of his soul. "I'm sorry that I've made you think I could do something like that, even for a second."

Then and there, Emelia got one thing straight. Drake

had passion for the words he spoke. He hadn't studied the *Romancing Women for Dummies* handbook that her ex-fiancé had apparently lived by, where a guy was allowed to say anything to get a woman in the sack. The gleam in Drake's eyes was hard, yet honest. As though he'd never whispered words holding more truth. Drake was a different breed. A rare creature in the social jungle—a man who stood up for a woman, despite her calling him evil a week earlier.

He was an accomplice to murder, Emelia reminded herself, and the man who would put her out of business. How could she forget so easily? Seemed the more she stared into his dark, brooding eyes, the more he made her forget the reason she was here.

"Sleaze or not," Emelia said, desperate for fresh air, "there was no reason for you to get all stabby on my thigh. We should've already been at the police station reporting what happened."

She turned her back on him and marched around a set of leather couches to the opposite end of the great room. Even though she'd put space between them, Drake's gaze bore into her back, heating her through and through. He slid behind her insanely fast, grabbed her hand, and spun her around.

"We can't go to the police. The report will become public record. Do you know what the media would do to me if they got wind of the situation? They'd twist the story into some kind of bar fight that spilled into the street."

Of course they would. It's what the media always did. Rat-race journalism had sprouted horns over the last few years, and from what Emelia could recall from Seattle's past headlines, they'd never had any dirt on Drake Wilder, rumored playboy. They would probably kill for details about a drunken bar fight, especially if they had the 411 from a "reliable source." If Emelia wanted to royally screw Drake over, this was the chance she'd been waiting for. His reputation would swirl down the tubes.

She couldn't do it. She couldn't destroy everything he'd worked for in one quick swoop, then pretend it wouldn't bother her in the slightest to do so.

She wasn't like him.

"The media couldn't twist anything if I told them how I was attacked by that guy, and how you saved me," she said quietly, taking back her hand. Tingly sensations lingered on her palm, flittering through her fingers and up her arm. She rubbed her hand on her jeans. Drake noticed, watching the swiping movement with grimly lit eyes.

"You think your statement would matter?" His voice lowered to a flat calm. "The media are in the money business, not the truth business."

Emelia folded her arms, hardening herself for a possible confession. "What happened to the biker?"

"Mr. Bloomfield took care of him," Drake said simply.

"What does that mean?"

"It means you don't have to worry about that guy, or anyone else, attacking you ever again. Mr. Bloomfield ran his background and discovered that he had a dozen warrants out for his arrest. We simply helped capture a wanted felon. Your attacker is behind bars at this very moment."

"Oh." Tension eased from Emelia's shoulders. She took comfort in the fact that she'd been wrong—Drake hadn't killed the biker. He wouldn't be charged with murder and she wouldn't have to testify about the attack in some godawful trial. To top it off, the greaseball wouldn't be attacking any other women in the future. "Well, that's...good, I guess."

Did the fact that her attacker was a felon make Drake any less shady for what he did? He protected her though, didn't he? And he clearly hadn't taken advantage of her, which he totally could have while she was knocked out. Maybe his motives were truly genuine. And maybe the sickeningly wealthy lived under the radar like this all the time, handling things quickly and efficiently so the media wouldn't be able to dig up any dirt.

"You hit the steering wheel pretty hard," he said. "How do your ribs feel?"

"They don't hurt much." Absentmindedly, Emelia touched her stomach, just below her breasts. Twinges of hollow, aching pain echoed through her. Sucking in a shallow breath, Emelia looked down and for the first time noticed a purple bruise forming on her chest, just below the lacy ridge of her tank top. "Shit, guess I hit harder than I thought."

"You should probably see a doctor." Drake's entire body stiffened like one of his statues.

"I bruise easy," she said. "It's the pale skin."

Drake responded with a clench of his jaw and a slow nod of his head. Emelia couldn't explain it, but she got the feeling he wanted to apologize for something. It couldn't be the apology Emelia hoped for, the one she deserved for putting up with his bullshit about the deed to her building, because he didn't know the true reason she'd taken the job at his company. He'd obviously screwed so many people out of their small business that he couldn't remember their names.

Why was he looking at her that way? She needed to get out of his house so she could think without feeling that Drake was studying her every move. Emelia eyed the door, wondering where she'd go when she walked through it. "Where's my car and all my stuff?"

"Your things are in the closet in the foyer. Your car is at EC's Tow and Repair. They'll have the damage fixed by the end of next week."

"Wonderful," she said, crossing the marble entry beneath a teardrop-shaped chandelier. Now she had to waste money on a rental, when she should be using it on legal fees to figure out the dilemma with Wilder Financial. As she thought about the possibility of being stuck in a lawsuit with Drake over the true and rightful ownership of her bar, a strange sensation tugged deep within her chest. It wasn't guilt. Couldn't be. She pulled her coat, purse, and phone from the closet, then flicked her phone to life and searched for a cab company to get home.

"You're welcome to drive one of my cars until yours is fixed."

"No, I don't think that's a good idea." Somewhere in his mansion, Mozart began to play, trickling soft notes into the foyer. "Thanks, but that's not necessary. I should go."

In a flash of movement, Drake blocked the door, outstretching his hand as if he had no intention of letting Emelia leave. She gasped, stopping as his palm brushed over her stomach. Pinpricks of heat bloomed over her skin. His chest was a wall of thickly corded muscle, his eyes a luxurious shade of honey-brown.

"I'd feel better knowing you weren't taking a cab to and from work," he said.

What did she care about making him feel better?

"I'll rent a car." Emelia covered the hand he'd placed over her stomach, and kneaded her fingers between his. Raw, animalistic hunger flickered across Drake's expression…until Emelia lifted his hand and returned it to his side. "But thanks for the offer."

"Emelia?" His gravelly voice laced with hints of pain.

She froze, staring at the notches in the ancient wood door, unable to look at him. The chemistry sparking between them was fierce and palpable, speeding her breathing. She couldn't afford to feel any of those things, so she stared straight ahead, channeling a faceless, emotionless zombie.

"What?" she said finally, failing miserably at the whole zombie thing.

"I already have a car waiting out front." He leaned down, his breath warm on her neck. "Considering you're bruised and just waking up from a long sleep, I think it's best that I drive you home…for safety reasons."

As he pulled back, Emelia glared, her lips twisting as annoyance bubbled inside her. She should've told him to buzz off, but before she could open her mouth to fight him on the issue, Drake put a finger to her lips, shushing her. The pad of his finger was surprisingly calloused for a guy who pushed papers all day, but the pressure against her skin was soft. Gentle. His finger reminded Emelia of his kiss, the way his lips moved against hers in a sensual caress. He took back his finger like she'd burned him. Then blocked the entire doorway, his arms folded over his chest.

"You're not leaving this house until you agree to let me drive you home." Two stalemated beats. "Emelia, say yes."

Drake may've been used to controlling things in the boardroom, but he wouldn't control her. Not now. Not ever. She stood tall and raised her chin so that she looked down her nose at him. "Make me."

His nostrils flared as he picked her up and tossed her over his shoulder like she weighed no more than a bag of feathers. She squealed, kicking her feet as he swept through the front door. Despite his speed and strength, Drake seemed oddly aware of where Emelia hurt—not a single hint of pain struck her as he bent her over his shoulder and carried out the door. She was strapped into the passenger seat of a black Mercedes, her stuff flung onto her lap, before she could argue.

For the first time in Emelia's life, she was struck speechless.

Chapter Seven

Clouds rolled in Monday morning, encasing the entire city in thick plumes of mist and fog. Drake wasn't in the mood to get down to business quite yet, and the dreary weather wasn't helping to motivate him. After Raul pulled files on the Knight Owl, the building on Porter Street, and Emelia Hudson's past, all Drake could think about was cornering Emelia the instant she stepped off the elevator.

They had to talk, to straighten things out regarding the building, and how he came to purchase it. He was certain that's why she was mad at him. Drake read the e-mails she'd sent. She'd been wrong on all counts regarding her deed and wouldn't listen to reason. Since she wouldn't quit with the e-mails, all messages past the first dozen had been sent straight to Raul's spam folder. He could've answered an e-mail or two, but it wouldn't have mattered legally. The facts were black and white.

Once they hashed things out, once Emelia saw the deed to her building in Drake's hand, he had questions for her. Questions about something personal that Raul discovered—

she'd applied for a marriage license one month before taking the job at Wilder. She'd accepted a proposal of marriage. In Drake's pack, that meant that she was off-limits. Untouchable.

What happened to her fiancé? Public records didn't show a marriage and she'd never mentioned it. The whole thing didn't sit right with him. His coffee tasted bland, though that could've been because he came in early and made it himself, and his coat clung to his shoulders too tightly.

As Drake strode around the last corner and spotted Emelia slumped over her keyboard, he cleared his throat. She gasped, nearly jumped out of her chair. "Drake? I—"

"In my office," he said, shoving open the office door. They needed to get the deed business over with so they could move on to more pressing things. Like when she'd been claimed by another.

"I wasn't sleeping, I swear," Emelia said, following his every step. "I was thinking…with my head down."

"I don't care." He strode to the windows and went palms-down on the glass. The cold lancing through his fingers did little to soothe the possessiveness flaring in his gut.

"I should get back out there."

"Stay," he commanded and then on second thought, added, "Please."

"I'm not supposed to leave my desk." Her voice wavered with uncertainty. "What if someone calls or comes in?"

"Let Trixie take the calls," Drake spun around, holding his breath as he brushed past her.

"Trixie's not here. She had to run an errand downstairs."

"We're going to straighten out this mess with your bar," Drake said, laying everything on the table. "And we're going to do it now."

Emelia stood in the center of his office, her mouth gaping as if he'd surprised her. She owned the hardworking secretary image with black dress pants that stove-piped to the floor, and a baby-blue sweater with crinkles of extra fabric at the collar. She was a chameleon, Drake gave her that much, able to adapt to the secretary role as easily as she had the bartending one.

"I know I said we should talk in the morning, but maybe we should talk about this later…when you don't look like you're about to kill someone." She took a step toward him, hesitating when he put his hands up to stop her. It was better if she didn't get too close—he wouldn't be intoxicated by her sugary sweet scent that way. "There's more bothering you than you're saying. What's going on?"

What *was* going on? Drake's entire body was drawn tight, a rubber band stretched to the limit. Barely holding on to the thread of composure, Drake strode to his desk and flipped open a manila envelope filled with copies of e-mails between her and Raul. "When do you claim to have bought the building on Porter Street?"

"When do I *claim* to have bought it?" Emelia mocked. She coughed out a laugh. "Good choice of words. Way to rob me of my bar in one fell swoop. I own that building. The Knight Owl is mine."

"When did you buy it and from whom?"

"Eight years ago, January." Folding her arms over her chest, Emelia sighed, then set her gaze on his mouth. "I bought it from the guy who owned the tattoo parlor next door. I'd leased from him for years, and one day he dropped in and showed me the deed to the entire building. He said the county rezoned and informed him that he could split off the bar from the tattoo parlor. He asked for fifty grand."

"Quite the steal, even for a building in that rough neighborhood." Drake circled his desk and perched on the edge, crossing his feet at the ankles. It staved off the urge to kick something. Barely. "So you just handed it over?"

With a cynical string of laughs, Emelia plopped into the leather seat facing him. He fought to keep his eyes level with hers and off the cleavage revealed from the drooping slouch of her sweater. His heart continued to race, meddling with his logic.

"You forget there are people who work years to make that kind of money." Emelia paused, and then, "I cut corners where I could, eating ramen and macaroni and cheese for months on end. I pinched pennies, couponed, worked sixteen-hour days, opening up the bar early for karaoke nights or live bands. I advertised. I sweat and bled. I was the owner, the accountant, the janitor, the historian, the hostess…I was everything. When it wasn't enough, I took side jobs waitressing during the day. It was damn hard, but I still couldn't save enough. The rest of the balance I put on credit cards."

Shit, Emelia was in deeper than he thought. "Why not get a loan through a bank so the transaction would be legit?"

"He said he'd dock the sale price ten grand if I kept the banks out of it. He claimed to own the building free and clear, and had the deed to prove it, so why not? I paid him cash, and he handed me my deed. I thought I owned the place… until *you* sent me a notice claiming to have bought the entire building."

Emelia's accusations rang loud and clear. She believed that Drake had destroyed everything she'd worked for, everything she'd put her heart into. He remembered how she'd been in the bar—assertive and confident, proud that the place was built on her sweat and tears. She'd taken something that was sheer business and had made it personal. No wonder she hated him.

"We're going to get a couple things straight." Drake watched her cheeks redden, and waited for steam to seep from her ears, but the train raced on. "Wilder Financial sent you the notice of purchase, not me. The board holds a meeting, we look at groups of property that are worth more than the sale price, I approve or deny the project, and it goes through.

We donate certain properties to the city and rebuild others. We go through banks. We check county records. Everything we do is by the book, all the time. If the scheme between you and Tattoo Parlor Guy didn't pan out, that has little to do with me or Wilder Financial."

"You ass." She stood with the spirit of a fighter—a short, spunky, blue-eyed featherweight who'd pull a muscle before she hurt someone.

If Drake wasn't drawn so tight, he might've laughed at the contrast between the softness of Emelia's appearance and the feisty show she put on. If she were a wolf, Drake thought, she'd be petite, with lean muscles and a sleek stride. A young wolf who thought she could snarl and growl and raise the fur on the back of her neck to frighten away packmates, even though they could take her down with the strike of a paw.

"You *are* Wilder Financial," she roared, standing up on tiptoe to better see him eye to eye. "The building has your name on it, for fuck's sake!"

Drake watched her chest heave, and nearly tasted the breath pushing past her lips. Biting back a hiss, Drake's feet lurched forward of their own accord. He stopped himself before he crashed into her. She eyed his lips with dark hunger, and for a sliver of a moment, Drake thought she was going to kiss him.

"Just because Wilder Financial has the deed doesn't mean *I* bought your bar," Drake forced out in a single, tight breath. "It means my corporation bought it."

He could give it back to her. The thought streamed through his head like a jetliner, and was gone as quickly as it had come. The entire area was in an economic downward spiral. If he gave the bar back to her, it wouldn't be long before the Knight Owl went bankrupt along with the rest of the small businesses in the area. At least if Wilder's City Beautification team got their teeth into it, there could be a chance to bring more business to the area, and to her bar.

Looking at the numbers—which is what Drake did best—there was only one way Emelia's bar was going to survive. Wilder Financial had to keep ownership of it.

"You are an expert at dodging things, aren't you?" Emelia fired. "You dodge e-mails, phone calls, and probably relationships, too, which would explain why you were in the cellar the night of the party instead of upstairs with everyone else. It doesn't matter anyway, because you didn't buy shit, not really."

"If you leave it alone, and let my company keep ownership, I think you'll find it'll help business. We have the backing to improve the building and the surrounding area. We could build the Knight Owl into twenty Knight Owls spread across the city. It could be better for everyone this way."

"You've never sweated and slaved for a piece of something that everyone else saw as worthless, have you? It's not about making buckets of cash or making the Knight Owl into a chain, it's about having something that's mine, something I clawed for, tooth and nail."

Damn, he admired her tenacity, but she wasn't getting it. Given the circumstances, the best option was for Wilder Financial to hold the deed. It was the better move, even if she didn't think it.

"I think you have to sue Tattoo Parlor Guy to get your money back." Drake could smell the sugar from Emelia's morning coffee on her breath—two sugars, one hazelnut cream. She'd taste just as sweet without the additives, Drake knew firsthand. "The deed to the Porter Street property that you have in your possession is fake, docu-edited, and worthless. Wilder Financial will hold the true deed in good hands until you're in a better position to make an offer."

There. He did it. Laid all the facts on the table.

"I have the deed to *my* building back at *my* bar, and

believe me, it's legit." Disdain darkened Emelia's eyes to deep-sea blue. She swayed against him as if the ground beneath her feet wobbled, then pulled back. "If you want me to drive across town and get it, just so you can see that it's the real deal, I can."

Somehow, the energy crackling between them flipped on a dime. Anger turned to something fiercely sexual, a hunger that clawed its way through him. As the temperature elevated from heated to scorching, Emelia swayed into him once more, nearly pressing against his chest. Drake fought the urge to kiss her, to taste the fire of her words and feel the spark on her skin. If Drake didn't release some tension soon—either by kissing her or kicking her out of the building—he was liable to spontaneously combust.

Drake didn't want Emelia to move a single inch, let alone drive across town to retrieve her fake deed. He wanted her to stay right where she was, a breath away from him, lips pouting in annoyance, cheeks flushing in anger. He wanted to piss her off and bottle the outpouring of emotion. She was different from him in every way—passionate where Drake was levelheaded, soft and curvy where he was achingly hard.

The wolf inside Drake shivered and shook, trembling with deep-rooted desire. It demanded to bond with Emelia, to claim what was rightfully his.

Mine.

"Why are you looking at me like that?" Emelia's plump lips quirked.

"Like what?"

"Like you want to eat me."

Ah, hell.

Now all Drake could think about was how the most intimate part of her body would taste. He went rock hard at the thought of sliding his fingers through her rich cream, then suckling them into his mouth. Drake could sense excitement spreading through Emelia like a blush, as if the shudder rushing through her were his own. He could almost feel her hot, velvety center on his tongue. Impulses to rip the clothes from her body and bend her over the desk shot like liquid fire through his veins.

One kiss would quench the fire burning inside him. They wouldn't sleep together—he wouldn't let it get that far. At least not until she knew what he was, and what place she could have in his world. But he couldn't stand here, enveloped in Emelia's scent, drunk on the sight of her lips and the smoldering behind her eyes, without sampling a sliver of the forbidden fruit.

One taste wouldn't hurt anything.

"You're not Little Red anymore," Drake said, his voice scratchy and deep, sounding strange to his own ears. "I'll only eat you if you ask me to."

Emelia gasped, her sapphire eyes blazing with dark desire. It was all the invitation he needed. He yanked her into his arms and branded a kiss on her mouth. The primal instincts bubbling inside him caught fire from the impact as his tongue darted past her lips and explored the warm, wet recesses of her mouth. He drank her in, sucking the sweetness from her lips.

"Emelia," he whispered, savoring the chills gathering at the base of his spine. "You're going to drive me crazy."

She smiled and nipped at his bottom lip. "About time."

She crashed into him then, from lips to hips. Looping her arms around his neck, Emelia dug her fingers through Drake's hair and deepened the kiss, pressing her breasts against his chest until their bodies couldn't be any closer without joining as one.

Hard rods of lust speared through Drake's gut, shattering his intentions and sense of duty. He needed to tell her that he was a werewolf, an Alpha, before she got too deeply involved.

She should know what could happen if they slept together. But none of that mattered. Not in this moment. Barbs of pure white heat crackled through every vein, throbbed through every muscle, and drew his erection painfully tight.

He hadn't imagined the spark behind Emelia's kiss in the cellar, though he tried to convince himself he had. Emelia was a tidal wave of scorching heat, her mouth a heaven that Drake explored with generous sweeps of his tongue.

He needed more of this. Less dry, rational thought. He coiled his arms around her tiny waist and scooped her off her feet. Keeping their lips fused together, Drake spun around and placed Emelia on the edge of his desk. She broke contact, only for a second. Shoved his entire desk spread to the floor. Scooted back and spread her legs. Desperate to touch her, to keep that spark firing in his gut, Drake wedged himself between Emelia's thighs. Her hair fell around her face and down to her shoulders, creating a golden mane that slipped through his fingers like strands of fine silk.

For a freeze-framed moment, Drake didn't care about the deed to a building on Porter Street or the fact that if Emelia turned into a werewolf, she'd never be able to have his children. There was only the sound of Emelia's rapid breathing and the hard pounding of his heart.

With a few swift tugs, Emelia loosened Drake's tie and unfastened the top buttons of his shirt. She pulled him down for another kiss, sliding her hips to the edge of the desk to meet him.

He kissed her harder, deeper, plunging his tongue into her mouth. Emelia met him stroke for stroke, and in one hard jerk, shoved his shirt down past his shoulders. On a moan, Drake tugged Emelia against him, her warm center flush against his straining shaft. He had to strip off her clothes and eliminate the cotton-blend barrier between them. He was desperate to feel the long spread of her legs wrap around him.

A symphony of knocks rapped on the door.

Brakes.

Emelia gasped, rolling off the desk as Drake backed away, stunned by what he—they—were about to do.

"One minute," he called out, shrugging into his shirt.

Scrambling to pick up the things she'd swiped to the floor, Emelia whispered something to herself that sounded like "way to go." After retying his tie and failing to hide his massive erection by pressing down the front of his slacks, Drake crouched and helped gather scattered pens and papers.

"I didn't plan for this to happen, I should've—"

"Sir," Raul said, pounding on the door twice more. "I've got Wilder Air on the phone and neither of your secretaries is out here to take the call. They need to know which jet you'd prefer to take to the Vanguard Gala."

Damn it. The charity event was this Saturday. He'd nearly forgotten.

He couldn't leave Emelia alone. Not when they still hadn't figured out which rogue group her attacker belonged to. He'd never live with himself if he left her behind and something horrible happened.

"Listen," he said, brushing her hand over a paper tray. "I have this thing going on Saturday night and I usually bring someone from the office along as my guest. Would you like to go with me?"

"I…umm…" Emelia shook her head as if she was in some sort of daze. "I don't think—"

"Sir, is everything all right?" Raul hollered.

"One minute!" Drake wrapped his fingers around Emelia's hand. Her skin was warm to the touch, buzzing through his palm. Would the connection between them ever fade? "It's a business function with a lot of people from the San Francisco office. It'll probably be a bore, but at least it'll get you out of Seattle for the weekend. Have you ever been to the city?"

She shook her head, sending blond tendrils of hair tumbling past her shoulders. He couldn't wait to see what she looked like glammed up. She'd be radiant. Showstopping. On second thought, they'd be in a crowded ballroom with hundreds of men gawking at her. He'd claw out every eyeball that veered her way. Drake clamped down on the possessive surge before it got him in trouble.

"The city's beautiful; you'd love it." Thankful his slacks no longer pitched at the groin, Drake stood and helped Emelia to her feet. "Say you'll come with me."

Staring as if she couldn't believe what was happening, Emelia's lips parted into what Drake read as a "yeah"…but no words came out.

"Is that a yes?"

More knocks. One slow nod.

It was a date…probably the most important one of his life.

Chapter Eight

Emelia was officially the dumbest woman on the planet. She was stupid. Beyond stupid. Mortifyingly, horrifyingly, moronically...*stupid*.

She stared at the deed she'd bought from Jared "Needles" Branch and fought to keep her mouth from gaping. Even now, five days after she'd realized that it was a fraud and that she'd been taken for a ride, her stomach still soured. She'd been so proud of the damn thing that she'd made a color copy, framed it, and hung it in the back room of the Knight Owl.

Tearing the garbage up and spitting on its pieces—and then in Needles's ugly, tattooed face—never sounded so good.

Drake had been a gentleman after their meeting on Monday, smiling softly as he whisked in and out of the office, asking her politely to get his coffee or make a few office-supply runs. Even when Emelia had marched into his office, bright and early Tuesday morning, with her deed clutched in her fist, he'd been polite. Talked to her without the snide remarks that existed before.

Finally, he'd given her what she'd wanted all along:

common decency.

He'd even brought in someone from the county with commercial plot maps and sale histories, and a banker with the transaction records to back his claim. All Emelia had was a piece of paper and the word of a lying snake.

Queen Stupid, at Drake's service.

After her ex ditched her at the altar, Emelia should've known better than to trust men. Especially ones who had their eyebrows replaced by arching tribal tattoos. It was that fact alone—that somewhere deep inside, she knew better—that had her apologizing to Drake for her rude comments the next day. He didn't mock her, laugh in her face, or berate her as she'd expected him to…as she would've done in his position. Instead, he'd said, "It was simply a miscommunication. Don't give it another thought."

Drake Wilder had a heart after all.

He'd even said he would sell it back to her when she was on her feet, after she sued Needles for her money back. Things were looking up.

As the elevator dinged, indicating someone had reached the top floor, Emelia fed her deed into the shredder, and suddenly remembered all those papers she'd destroyed of Drake's the first day.

"Shit." Her gaze shifted to Trixie's desk. How could she find out what those papers were and replace them? Drake might've been content with her for the time being, but when he found out what she did, he'd be livid.

"Your dress came," Trixie said, barreling around the corner swinging a black garment bag.

"Oh yeah? Bring it here." Emelia cleared a spot for the dress as Trixie laid it out and waited impatiently for Emelia to give it the unzip.

Emelia had tried to forget about the Vanguard Gala all week, but Drake's reminder e-mails didn't help. She felt foolish, and wasn't looking forward to bathing in uncomfortable silence all weekend. She'd been ridiculous for fighting a point she should've known to be false. She'd apologized. Drake had accepted her apology. Still, Emelia's behavior was inexcusable. She'd shredded his documents, conveniently forgotten to relay messages, and had even started switching his black coffee for decaf, little by little, hoping he would be groggy and unmanageable in front of his business associates.

To make matters worse, Drake had been so damned kind through the whole thing. He'd been disgustingly... *understanding*.

She had to make it up to him somehow. She would be the best date he'd ever brought to the Vanguard Gala, on her best behavior.

"What are you waiting for?" Trixie asked.

"I don't know." Nerves danced in Emelia's veins, and tingled through her arms. "Maybe I should wait to put it on until I get home."

"Oh no, you're not going to deny me this. If you're not going to be excited about it, I'll do it for you. Mr. Wilder always picks the attire for this event. Last year he bought me a McLourdes, the most expensive and elegant on the line. It was silver and flowing with diamonds at the collar." Trixie smiled as if she wore the dress now, and seemed to glow from its memory. It should've been a crime for a woman to have brains, sensibility, *and* beauty that rivaled a model's. "Aren't you even a little anxious to see what he got you?"

Emelia hadn't gotten dressed up for a formal event in years...since prom, probably. While she'd always loved to dress up, she'd never found an excuse, and had never had a boyfriend who would agree to take her somewhere that required it.

"Yeah," she shrugged, playing down her feelings. "I guess."

Staring at the long, black bag, Emelia couldn't squelch

the excitement that bubbled in her belly. Drake could afford to buy from the most expensive stores on the planet. They were attending a benefit gala in San Francisco, a place she'd always dreamed of going. There were going to be celebrities at the event, Wilder coworkers from across the country, and *Forbes* businessmen. It was a black-tie affair, which meant anything could be in the bag: Gucci, Prada, Dolce & Gabbana. Emelia shuddered with anticipation as a single name streaked through her thoughts: *Vera*.

"Well, come on!" Trixie waved her hand impatiently. "Unzip it, or I will."

"All right." Emelia unzipped as Trixie peeled apart the bag opening.

"Oh my—" Trixie gasped, hand to mouth, as the zipper hit the bottom of the bag, revealing the entire dress.

"It's"—air wheezed past Emelia's lips—"pretty?"

The dress was a hodgepodge of cotton and lace, full length, flat black, and full-collared. It was perfect…for a nun in training. A blind nun. Who picked her own clothing. From Walmart.

"This has to be a mistake." Trixie backed away like the dress was covered in maggots. "I must've picked up the wrong bag from the designer."

Speechless, Emelia checked the tag. No mistake. The garb was hers. She pulled it out by its hanger and held it up, then met Trixie's mortified gaze. "Is this what women wear to these things?"

"Oh honey." Trixie's hand found Emelia's shoulder as if she were consoling her after a death in Emelia's family. "What has gotten into that man?"

Things never worked out as Emelia dreamed. She should've been used to that by now.

"If this is what Mr. Wilder wants me to wear, I'll do it." She owed him at least that much. "It's just so…"

"Morticia Addams?"

"Uh-huh."

Gazing far off, Trixie twirled a strand of caramel-colored hair around her finger. "What time is Mr. Wilder picking you up tomorrow?"

"He's sending the limo to my place at noon. Why?"

"I want to know how much time I have to get Cinderella ready for the ball. Fairy godmothers don't work well under time crunches, you know."

"Maybe I shouldn't mess with it. I mean, this is his event and I'm attending as his date." The word sent chills racing to her middle. "I wouldn't want to toss this aside and wear something different. I wouldn't want to…offend him."

She'd done enough of that already.

"Oh sweetie," Trixie exhaled, her full lips quirking into a smile. "If he wants you to wear black, we don't want to disappoint him. But if you leave everything else to me, I promise you that Mr. Wilder won't be offended by your new dress. Not one bit."

Something mischievous sparked behind Trixie's eyes. Emelia stared at the black burlap sack flattened across her desk, and although she had no idea what Trixie had in mind, it couldn't be worse than *that*.

"Okay," Emelia said, with a decisive nod. "What's the plan?"

As Trixie put an arm over her shoulder and led her to the elevators, Emelia couldn't help but feel like this moment was a game-changer in a game she never really understood in the first place.

. . .

Drake's chest was going to implode. He checked his watch. Again.

One thirty.

When Drake had arrived at Emelia's apartment at noon, right on time, Emelia had told him she was running late and asked if he wouldn't mind waiting downstairs for a few minutes.

An hour and a half was more waiting than he could afford. With the ride to the airport, flight time, and the ride to the gala, they were already pushing it. While he hated parties, galas, and benefits where stares and whispers were the norm, he couldn't be late to this one. The Vanguard Gala had always been special to him, and he needed to get there early to make sure everything was in order, the way he'd arranged it. He'd ordered his top packmates to guard the hall in the case there was another attack. They should've been there already, waiting for his orders.

With a huff and one last glance at his watch, Drake pushed off the limo and strode across the sidewalk. And stopped in his tracks when he spotted the most beautiful woman he'd ever seen descend from the stairs ahead of him.

A stunning black dress hugged Emelia's curves, sucking against her breasts and hips. Layers of soft black fabric flared at the knee like billowing flowers falling to the ground. Her body was covered in stripes of black and beige, although the beige made it look like she was nude beneath stringy black fabric, which made Drake's stomach tighten with anxiety. As Drake raised his gaze up the floral neckline to Emelia's shimmering pale lips and dark, smoke-colored eye makeup, he realized the night was definitely not going to go as planned. He stared so long without blinking that his eyes dried and stuck to his lids. He rubbed them quickly and licked his lips to return the moisture.

"Sorry for making you wait," she said, once she'd reached the sidewalk. She did a little spin, revealing her exposed back and the bunching black fabric that gathered just above her rear. "What do you think?"

Good god. Her back was tan and smooth, her shoulders rounded with silken muscle dropping to a tiny, sexy waist.

He couldn't formulate a coherent sentence if he tried, so he nodded and swallowed down the desire to tell her how absolutely exquisite she looked. How he was so proud that she would be on his arm tonight.

"What happened to the other dress?" The one he'd chosen to ensure no other men would get any crazy ideas about stealing his date. Drake swallowed cotton balls. "The, uh, black one."

Emelia shrugged, her bare shoulders tapping loose tendrils of blond curls that dangled from the coil on the back of her head. "This one's black, too, in case you didn't notice."

He'd noticed every last detail. The way her eyes shone a richer shade of blue, like the Aegean Sea after a drizzling rainstorm. He drank in the lean lines of her body, memorizing every last detail, every subtle curve.

How much longer was he going to be able to hold back from her? He'd planned on telling her everything when the time was right, but it seemed every time they got close, there was something between them—the deed issue, the biker, the questions about her fiancé. Normally, time wouldn't have been an issue. He could've introduced Emelia to his world slowly, so the adjustment period would be smooth and manageable. But the longer Drake waited, the more their connection increased. It was like a magnet had taken up residence in their chests and sucked them together when they were close. He couldn't take things further until she knew the truth. He couldn't deceive her that way, yet he couldn't seem to keep his hands off her, either.

And he couldn't help but think about where their relationship was headed. She was *human.* Even if she found out about their world and accepted it, she would have to know she could never have children and a family. Not if she bonded with him.

He'd always wanted an heir. Had always wanted someone to take over the pack when he was old and out of his prime. But he'd wanted to have a partner in life and love as well. Maybe only having one of those things would be enough…

"You look amazing," he said, opening the door of the limo. "Who do I have to thank for your last-minute wardrobe change?"

She settled into the seat, Drake beside her, and they were off.

"Trixie thought the occasion called for a bit more flair."

Drake huffed, hiding the swell in his pants with his tuxedo coat. "I bet she did."

They drove to the airport, talking the entire way about what to expect for the evening. Emelia needed to know this was business first, pleasure second, and that there would be heightened security measures at the hall. He assured her it was all for precautionary purposes.

She believed every word of it.

The limo pulled into the airport and passed a few guard stations, then stopped in front of a private jet. The stairs had been pulled down and a red carpet had been laid out.

"Hold the phone. We're taking this?" Emelia asked, peering beneath the doorframe. Her perfume was rich and sweet, smelling like warm honey melted over vanilla, and wafted around Drake as she leaned over to get a better look. "This is intense."

He'd been thinking the same thing.

"I can guarantee the night will only get more intense from here," he said, and had no idea how he was going to handle it.

Chapter Nine

City hall was breathtaking in its grandeur, the perfect place to host the Vanguard Gala. Lightly toned granite and sandstone gave the inner rotunda an elegant, American Renaissance feel, from the larger-than-life pillars to the intricate archways, to the grand staircase. Round tables and cloth-covered chairs filled the entire circular hall, with robust flower arrangements in every corner and on every table. Purple and red auras of light focused on the wall above the staircase and in the center of the dance floor added impressions of sophistication familiar to the Wilder Foundation.

Emelia looped her arm through Drake's and moved around the room like a goddess, with her shoulders pulled back and chin held high. If she was nervous, she didn't show it. It didn't matter if Drake introduced her to the mayor of San Francisco or the woman who coordinated the event, Emelia radiated kindness, jumping into effortless conversation with everyone who crossed her path.

Even though Drake had heightened security inside city hall, he couldn't shake the nerves rattling his bones. Emelia wasn't out of harm's way yet. Whoever sent the goon to attack her would be back. Luckily, his packmates were in top form, on high alert, searching for anything out of order. Emelia had Drake's full, undivided attention.

After swiping two flutes of champagne off the tray of a passing server, Drake escorted Emelia around the room and up the stairs to the balcony that overlooked the bustling hall below. He'd ordered three of his best men to follow Emelia everywhere she went. Even now, they kept pace behind them, far enough away that they couldn't overhear conversation, but close enough to jump into action if something happened.

As the murmur of the guests washed over them, Emelia leaned against the nearest balcony and peered over the side. "You never told me what the gala is celebrating."

"You never asked." Drake tipped back his glass, not sure how much he wanted to tell Emelia. Although he longed to tell her everything, there was a very fine line between revealing just enough and too much. One small word could tip the balance. Too much, she'd get scared and bolt. Drake couldn't protect her that way. That was the last thing he wanted.

"This is me asking," she said.

Drake stepped beside her, scanning the crowd for someone out of place. "Serephina Vanguard was a visionary, donating most of her money to the city's performing art programs, museums, and parks, when people didn't have money to support such ventures. She even helped build the city's first opera house. She understood that there was more to a city than the people who governed it, a kind of inspirational river that flowed through it, influencing the people who lived there. She believed that the heart of a prosperous society comes from individuals who are creative thinkers, people who challenge established beliefs. She was a revolutionary, hated by some who thought her money should go toward more practical things…like government and election campaigns."

"So, aside from donating to creative programs in San Francisco, she bucked the system? Sounds like my kind of lady." Emelia nodded as if she understood, but had no idea. "Will she be here?"

Drake took another hearty drink, trying to drown the memory. "No, she passed away years ago."

Drake ached to tell her the truth about Serephina Vanguard. He didn't know why—he'd never wanted to reveal the truth to any of the other women who'd come in and out of his life in the last three hundred years. Emelia was different. She didn't act like everyone else, respecting him because of his authority in the pack or his position in the company. She treated everyone equally whether they worked the mail room or owned the company. She reminded him of Serephina in that way. It was clear Drake had to earn her respect; he planned on doing just that.

"Wilder Financial donates millions of dollars every year to keep the Vanguard Foundation going strong," he said. "It's one of the things I'm most proud of. This gala is to thank the people who keep Serephina's memory alive."

Emelia looked at him. Really looked at him. As if she could see the man behind the black-and-white penguin suit, the man who wanted Wilder Financial to be more than a multimillion-dollar corporation. His senses picked up the soft hint of fondness—it bloomed off Emelia in waves, peaceful and hesitant, like a flower opening its petals after a long winter.

"Funny how women who are scoffed at for forward thinking are revered after they're gone," she said.

Drake nodded, needing to say more, aching to connect the bridge spanning between them. Things he shouldn't say lingered on his tongue and burned a hole in his throat. How could he tell her that he was a werewolf? That he'd be the luckiest werewolf alive if she ruled the pack with him? Might as well sign him up for *Maury*. He'd fit right in on the "My Boyfriend Is a Freak" show.

As the gala's host tapped the microphone, announcing that everyone should take their seats, Drake leaped, saying the words he had never spoken to another.

"Serephina was my mother. Vanguard was her maiden name."

"Really?" Emelia's smoky eyes widened in surprise. She touched his arm gently, and smiled. "And here I thought you came from heartless parents who fought for big businesses and accounted little for people's feelings."

"You never cease to amaze me." He shook his head. "Why don't you tell me how you really feel?"

"I'm not sure what I feel, actually." Emelia closed the distance between them and placed both her hands on his shoulders. "But I know it's slowly changing."

"*Please take your seats*," the Vanguard Foundation representative blared over the microphone. He'd been chosen to host the gala not only for his role in the company, but for his Barry White baritone. "*The reception is about to begin*."

Drake braced himself as floodgates of desire burst open inside him. His hands found Emelia's waist and he tugged her against him, cherishing the feel of her body against his. This was how it should be always—the two of them together. The thought struck Drake like a drum, vibrating through his body. He wanted to bond with her, bury himself deep inside her, and live every day of his life making her glow with happiness.

But would it be enough if she couldn't give him children? Would his pack respect him anyway? God, he wished the answers were easier to understand. He wanted to believe that it didn't matter. That he'd control the pack without an heir just fine. But it did matter on some level. His father had beaten the concept of pack pride into him since he was young enough to understand. His father had also been the one to tell him that turned werewolves were not strong enough to fit with the rest…

"When I first met you I thought there was nothing to you," Emelia whispered. "I thought you were cold and merciless, chopping small businesses off at the knees for your own selfish gain. But you're not that way at all, not really."

"No," he said, catching the sincerity in her gaze. "Not really, but don't tell anyone. You'd ruin my bad-boy image."

His skin warmed beneath her hands, radiating through his chest. He could kiss her, right here, right now. She was so close, her lips parting in supple invitation. He couldn't speak, couldn't breathe.

"I think it's easy for people to mistake your keen business sense for harshness, but there's more to you than meets the eye." She leaned in close, until Drake's stomach tumbled. "Certain times, like in the cellar, in your office, and right now, I feel warmth brewing inside you. I think you pretend to be cold so no one gets close."

"You're close now," he said against her lips.

"I am." Her breath hitched as her gaze drifted down his chest. "And I like what I feel."

Hot-blooded impulses fired in Drake's middle, dizzying him. He braced himself on the balcony behind Emelia and guided her against the railing. She smiled, anticipating the pressure of his body.

"Do they follow you everywhere?" Emelia asked, tilting her head at the guards, who were pretending not to watch their interlude.

He couldn't take his eyes off the plumpness of her lips. "They're here for your protection."

"My protection?" Her voice was a delicious whisper. "From who? You?"

"Maybe."

Why did he just say that? Because he was a werewolf and

she was a woman with no knowledge of their world? Damn it. If he didn't know better, he would say he'd just spoken the truth.

"Serephina Vanguard is the reason we are here tonight." The host's voice boomed from the hall as the hum in Drake's stomach amplified.

"I don't need to be protected from you, Drake. Not anymore. Come on." Emelia slipped from his hold and headed toward the stairs. "I don't want to miss this."

The host's voice continued to rumble through the hall as Drake escorted Emelia down the grand staircase and found their seats at the edge of the room. For the first time since he'd hosted the gala, Drake wondered how quickly he could slip out of the hall and take Emelia somewhere private.

"She was born in 1850 to a poor family from New York City and passed away in San Francisco in 1938. Serephina Vanguard had no children, and instead chose to donate her time raising the creative climate of San Francisco. Her legacy continues, only through the grace of supporters like you."

Drake pinched his eyes shut as he pushed in Emelia's chair, hoping she didn't pay attention to the details in the host's speech. The burn-through-his-skin glare Drake received when he sat beside Emelia proved his worst fears.

"You told me she was your mother." She leaned over without looking at him, and talked to his shoulder. "You either lied to me, or you're the most gorgeous elderly guy I know. Serephina died in the thirties."

"I'll explain everything," Drake said, as chills scampered down his neck, "but my introductory speech comes first."

She shot him a scowl, her eyes narrowing to slits. "What reason would you have to lie about something like that?"

The words were a hammer to the heart. Drake couldn't stand it anymore. When they hadn't yet ironed out the deed issue, Emelia thought Drake was a scoundrel. Now that he'd finally hurdled that obstacle, Emelia thought he was liar. He should've kept her upstairs until the host called his name. He could've pressed her against one of those pillars and kissed her until the only thing she could hear was the fevered rush of blood in her ears.

But no. Just when he got Emelia to trust him, he faced a disbelieving frown. Seemed they were destined to dance the one-step-forward, two-step-back tango.

"And now, may I introduce our man of the hour…"

"I didn't lie," Drake said, placing a hand on her knee. The urge to tell Emelia about what he really was, about the role she played in his life and his heart as his Luminary, struck him hard and true. That's it…he'd tell her everything tonight. Once they were alone. "I told you that I'd explain what's going on, and I will…after my speech. We'll go somewhere quiet where we can talk, and I'll tell you things I should've told you when we first met."

"…the man who is responsible for putting this evening together, the philanthropist who has donated more money to the Vanguard Foundation than all of our other supporters combined…"

"What kind of things?" Emelia asked, ducking as a spotlight swept over them. "What should you have told me?"

"Mr. Russell D. Wilder!"

Applause swarmed like bees as blinding spotlights homed in on Drake. In that instant, he became the burning ant beneath a sun-scorched magnifying glass. Every move he made was analyzed, every word dissected.

He smiled and waved. Like he'd been trained. "Promise that you'll stay right here," he said into Emelia's ear. "Stay here until I come back for you."

Taking his notecards from his pocket, Drake marched on stage and tried to focus on what he was doing this for… instead of the woman glaring at him from table five.

Chapter Ten

Why was she prone to canoodling with liars? The entire length of Drake's speech, Emelia thought back over everything he'd said. She believed him when he talked about Serephina Vanguard on the balcony. He'd looked sincere, almost pained, when he talked about her passing and how much he'd done for the project.

She needed fresh air. She needed a chance to think without thousands of eyes staring at her, wondering who she was and why she deserved to be here with Drake, the world's most eligible bachelor.

Emelia bolted the first chance she got, and that chance came thanks to Drake's bodyguards. When Drake's speech ended, a group of burly men grabbed him by the elbows and escorted him behind the stage. His bodyguards were the largest Emelia had ever seen, and easily the most handsome. Each of the men had razor-short hair, strong features, and surprisingly gentle eyes. Did he only hire former Abercrombie models or something?

Emelia hurried out the hall, down the outside steps, and

around the rectangular patch of grass that stretched before her as long and wide as a football field. Buzzing with life, the noise of the city blended into one constant roar, drowning out the thoughts screeching through her head.

She slowed as she reached the trees lining the grass and shivered with awareness.

Someone was watching her.

Was it one of Drake's guards? They seemed to be everywhere tonight. Always watching. Like they were waiting for something in particular. Something that had to do with her.

Keeping her pace slow, so that she wouldn't wander too far from the hall, Emelia became hyperaware that someone was closing in. A rogue draft of crisp night air hit the back of her neck, launching a goose bump assault over her entire body.

"Hello?" Emelia asked, slowly spinning, peering through the dark between the trees that lined the opposite end of the grass. "If you're looking for Drake, he's still inside."

Out of the shadows beside her, Drake appeared. Emelia jumped, clutching her heart.

"You scared the hell out of me," she said, fighting the urge to smack him.

"I didn't mean to frighten you." Drake's gait was slow and deliberate. Almost a stalk. "Enjoying the night?"

The tone of his voice was different. Warmer and deeper. Somehow, Emelia thought she picked up the hint of an accent. Was it Middle Eastern? Drake was gorgeous in a tux, his shoulders impossibly broad, accentuating the squareness and strength of his jaw and the trim cut of his waist.

Liar, she reminded herself. Why did he have to be so good-looking? It would be easier to hate him if he looked like a beast. "I was having a great time. I even felt like Cinderella for most of the night, until someone lied to me."

"Who could lie to such a beautiful creature?"

"Very funny." She quirked her head and walked past him. He wasn't going to pretend the lies didn't happen—she wasn't in the mood. "Did you think I'd look at you differently if I thought she was your mother?"

Drake seemed to stiffen, then fell into line beside her. "The truth is, I don't like thinking of my mother, not when she pretended to have good intentions while screwing her own family out of money that was rightfully theirs."

"Wow," she said, turning to face him. "So she is your mother? You're going with that story now?"

"She is my mother—at least she was before I disowned her. It's complicated. And like I said, I'd rather not talk about the witch."

"You sure know how to flip your words ass over end, don't you? One second you're singing Serephina's praises and the next you're throwing her under the bus. I'm sure you do the same thing with your women."

Oh, she had Drake's number now. She'd met men like him before. Hell, she'd almost married a man like him before. Emelia was dead tired of men flipping their minds and hearts like light switches. One second they were in love, the next they were fleeing to Las Vegas to marry the stripper from their bachelor party…not that she knew from experience or anything.

Drake's expression remained still as stone. He closed the distance between them, but kept moving as if he would run her right over if she didn't back up. The first pangs of fear hit Emelia's system hard and she retreated, backing against the trunk of a tree. Drake stayed on course, and didn't stop until his body was against hers, his knee wedged between her thighs. Alarms went off in Emelia's brain and she put her hands against his chest to stop him.

"What are you doing?" she said. "Back off."

This man looked like Drake, but he...*wasn't*. Her eyes may have been playing tricks on her by seeing double, but deep down she knew this man wasn't Drake. Same determined stare, same build and stature, but there was one tiny difference: this man didn't have a tiny indentation on his left ear.

"You're a stunner, I'll give Drake that much." The man's eyes churned with hatred. "I'm surprised he's been able to last as long as he has. If you were my Luminary, I would've had you ten times over already."

Definitely. Not. Drake.

Emelia tried to slide past Drake's look-alike. He pinned her in place, trapping both of her wrists in one of his hands. A shadow crossed over his face, turning his features sinister. She cried out, but he clamped a large hand over her mouth, severing her scream.

"You're going to get something through your head." His hot breath coated her face. "You're leaving with me tonight, and you're going to be my sweet little ticket to getting everything. If you come with me quietly, it'll be far less painful than what'll happen to you if you scream again."

If she could get to the street, she could scream to high heaven. Someone would have to help her. She might have a chance to get away. Where was Drake? Would he even know to look for her out here? And what happened to all those guards who were stationed everywhere? Couldn't any of them wander outside for a smoke? She'd been stupid to leave the gala. She should've stayed at the table like he'd told her to. Having no other choice, Emelia nodded, her lips mashed beneath the stranger's meaty fingers.

"Good girl." The stranger eyed Emelia curiously, his gaze settling on her lips. Slowly, he removed the hand from her mouth, but kept his knee firmly in place. "Why my brother hasn't taken advantage of this sweet body of yours, I'll never know. Has he told you why he hasn't completed the bond with you yet? Has he told you that you're not strong enough? That you'll never be like us?"

"Your *brother*? Completed the bond?" Confused as hell and rattled to the core, Emelia tried to stay strong, fighting against her natural reaction to shake like a leaf. She downright refused to play the part of a victim. "I don't know what you're talking about."

"Why hasn't he at least bitten you and started the transition? It's a shame to leave you so weak and vulnerable."

"Bitten me?" Emelia felt like she'd been warped into the twilight zone. This guy truly was a monster. "Keep your teeth away from me."

"He hasn't told you a thing, has he? It's a shame to leave you in the dark, especially since you're his Luminary." The stranger tsk'd his tongue against his blindingly white teeth. "You see, if I bit you right here"—his cold fingers brushed against her neck—"you'd start the transition process."

Emelia's breath hitched as his nails dug into her skin. He was a madman. Certifiably insane. She should scream. She should knee him in the crotch and run. Emelia's arms and legs grew heavy, frozen from fear.

"If I bit you in the exact same place, or left you with one only one bite, you'd die a long, painful death. But if I bit you on a second pulse point, right here for example"—his hand brushed Emelia's inner thigh through her gown—"you'd finish the transition and become one of us. But you won't get the chance to experience that kind of power rushing through your veins. I've got far greater plans for you than that."

Oh, God.

"You're going to be my ticket to ruling the pack I was always meant to rule. I was born first, damn it, the title was rightfully mine. But it's no matter now. Thanks to you, I'm getting everything." Bending down, the stranger inhaled deeply, then moaned. "Your fear smells so damn good. I could keep you here all day."

"I don't know anything about a bite or a transition or what you want from Drake. Let me go." Emelia wriggled against him, but it was no use. He was too large, too strong, and was holding her too tightly. The more she struggled, the more he pressed against her. "I think you have me confused with someone else. I'm not worth anything to Drake."

He laughed and brushed a rough hand down her cheek. "So beautiful, so naive. Too bad we can't stick around longer. I'd love to strip that innocent look off your face right along with this dress, but I can sense that some of his pups are on their way." As he removed his knee from between Emelia's thighs, his dark eyes glazed over. "Meet me at the corner. Ten seconds." His tone changed into something slithery and dark. He wasn't talking to her…but to whom, then?

"I'm not going anywhere with you."

"Oh, you're coming. Whether you're unconscious or not is up to you." His fingers gouged into the back of her neck like she was a disobedient dog as he dragged her toward the street. Emelia tugged against him, skidding her heels over the concrete. A black Suburban screeched to a stop at the corner and the rear passenger door kicked open. Two shadowed forms lurked inside.

Oh, hell no.

She fought against him harder, tried to rip his fingers off her neck, tugging and pulling at his arm. She tried to trip him, tangling her legs in his. Still, he dragged her as if she weighed nothing.

"Don't make me knock you out." He snatched the mound of hair on her head and pulled.

Emelia yelped, both hands flying to her head as he jerked her along. There wasn't much time. She'd taken enough self-defense classes to know that once she got in the SUV, she was good as dead.

Thinking fast, Emelia craned her neck around and yelled, "Drake!" as if she saw him coming.

It was enough to make the stranger turn. Emelia took the opening and kneed him in the crotch. He hit the ground, choking on air. She bolted. Through the trees. Across the grass. Her heels sunk in, slowing her pace, so she ripped them off.

"Help!" City hall was close, its pillars towering over her. They had to have a side door. "Somebody help me!"

Something slammed into Emelia from behind. She tripped, landing face-first in the wet grass. Piercing pain shot through her nose, making her eyes water and her temples throb. She flipped over, gasping as she stared into a pair of onyx-black, pissed-off wolf eyes. Emelia trembled, her breath pushing past her lips staccato and cold.

The wolf had Emelia pinned, one gigantic paw on either side of her head. Showing its razor-sharp teeth, the wolf growled and went rigid as if it was filled with rage. Fur on its head stood on end and its lips pulled back in a hideous snarl. Then, with a haunting howl that split the night, it bit into Emelia's neck. Jagged teeth sank in deep, pulling at tendon and muscle. Screams got lost in Emelia's throat as she gasped for air. The wolf tore its head from side to side, gnashing its teeth in her skin. Searing pain mixed with terror filled Emelia's body, from head to foot, blood to bone.

The wolf pulled back, its muzzle dripping in blood.

Her blood.

If I bit you in the exact same place, you'd die a long, painful death. The stranger's words echoed through her head as the wolf bared its canines and reared up. Emelia cringed and pinched her eyes tight, bracing for the wolf—or the man behind the wolf's eyes—to kill her.

From out of nowhere, a second wolf crashed into the first. Clutching the gaping wound on her neck, Emelia maneuvered herself around, scrambling over the grass. Two wolves circled round and round, snapping and snarling at one another. Only they didn't complete a full pacing circle. The darker of the two wolves, the one who'd saved her, didn't seem to want to let the other near her. As the lighter wolf leaped in Emelia's direction, the darker wolf growled and chomped at its neck. When the lighter wolf darted the opposite direction, the darker matched its flash of movement.

They were equal size—larger than pictures of wolves Emelia had seen—with thick black fur and hunched backs. They moved with the same deadly stealth and attacked with the same brute strength. They could've been the same wolf. Brothers, maybe.

Wait…hadn't the stranger called Drake his brother? Hadn't the wolf attacked Emelia seconds after she kneed the stranger in the family jewels? Beyond the wolves, the stranger was nowhere to be seen.

Couldn't be, yet the word resounded in Emelia's brain like a gong.

Brothers. Werewolves.

Chest constricting, Emelia crawled backward, her feet catching on the tail of her dress. She couldn't pry her eyes away from the gruesome scene in front of her. It was like a horrible car crash unfolding in slow motion. The darker wolf chomped into the lighter wolf's neck. It howled, then sliced its paws over the darker one's back. They tumbled, throwing each other aside, clambering to their huge paws, then attacking again.

As Emelia's vision blurred, she touched her neck and came away with a hand smeared with blood. It ran down her arm, red and thick, soaking the embossed petals in her dress. She was losing too much. She was going to bleed out on the grass in front of city hall. What a historic moment that would be!

Howls came from all around her—beside her, above her,

from the hall itself. The sound was loud and muffled, like a distant trumpet announcing battle. Emelia supposed she simply had to wait for the soldiers to arrive.

She tried to get to her feet and slipped as dizziness set in. Defeated by her lack of strength, Emelia clutched the cool lawn and pressed her face against it. The dampness of the grass somehow soothed her, calming her racing heart. One wolf—she couldn't tell which since their colors had blended together—glared at the other down its nose and growled so deeply that it shook the earth. The other wolf growled back, lower, though no less menacing, then took off running toward the black blur parked on the street.

It wasn't two shuddering breaths before Emelia was surrounded by howls and stomping feet. Her eyes fluttered closed as the sound of Drake's voice penetrated her weary haze. "It'll be all right, Emie. I promise I'll make everything all right."

Muffled barks.

"How'd she get out here alone?" Drake's voice. More growls. "You were supposed to be watching her every second. If she doesn't recover from this, I'll have your hide!"

Emelia's dress tore away. Misty night air danced across her exposed legs. A warm mouth pressed a kiss against her inner thigh before she was bitten a second time.

Chapter Eleven

A cool washcloth pressed against Emelia's forehead, jarring her awake. She gasped, sitting upright in a strange bed, in a strange room. Drake sat on a leather chair beside the bed, his face a dark mask. He looked tired—shadows hovered beneath his eyes and stress lines indented the corners of his mouth.

"Thank God you're awake. I was beginning to think you'd never wake up." Drake leaned back in his chair, though he still seemed on edge. "How do you feel?"

"Hungry. Tired. Achy." Like she'd been flattened by a steamroller. "Where am I?"

"After the gala I brought you to my house outside the city. It's the most heavily guarded home I have. Consider it your personal Fort Knox."

She felt safe with Drake, no matter if she slept in Fort Knox or his mansion in Seattle, but she appreciated the fact that he wanted to make her feel that way.

"Is your head pounding?" he asked, rubbing his hands down his slacks.

She winced, touching the back of her head. Memories of the gala fought to the forefront of her mind. Why couldn't she remember details from that night? Why was the event a blur after Drake's speech? "I feel like power drills are grinding into my skull."

"That's good, under the circumstances." Drake crossed his legs, bringing his ankle up over his knee, causing Emelia's concentration to blow apart.

She hadn't noticed until now: his tie was missing and his dress shirt was unbuttoned to his waist. As Drake shifted in his seat, the sides of his shirt fell away, revealing tan, sculpted muscle on his chest and downright lickable washboard abs. Despite herself, Emelia's tongue shot out over her lips.

"A power drill is playing tic-tac-toe on the back of my head. Remind me how that's a good thing?" She dropped her head back on the pillow and groaned. "My insides feel raw."

"Raul is bringing you some Tylenol along with breakfast. Is there anything you want in particular? I'll bring doughnuts if you promise not to practice your pitch on me."

"Very funny." As Emelia's stomach growled, a hunger pang ripped through her. "This is going to sound crazy, but I'd kill for deep-dish pizza. Too early?"

"Not at all." Drake laughed, the tension in his gravelly voice washing away. "I'll have Raul bring you the best pizza in the city."

His eyes glazed over and his head kinked to the side. Almost as though he floated somewhere in his mind. Then, in the next breath, he was back again, the same specks of worry shining in his eyes.

Suddenly, Emelia realized she wasn't wearing the dress from the gala. "What's this?" she asked, tugging on the collar of a men's white cotton T-shirt. The thing was huge, dwarfing her body and sagging over her shoulders.

"After I brought you here, I changed you out of your

gown. It had a few stains on it. I didn't peek." Smiling, Drake put up a hand in pledge. "Swear on the Bible."

"You probably don't even own a Bible."

"I washed your face," Drake continued, "and took down your hair. I thought you'd be more comfortable that way." He grabbed a bottle of water from the bedside table, unscrewed the top, and handed it to her. "Here, take it. I'm sure you're parched."

Drake was right—her throat was abnormally dry. Like she'd wolfed down a package of sandpaper. She meant to take a sip of the water, but couldn't stop guzzling once the water hit her throat.

"How long was I out?" she asked, handing back an empty bottle.

"It's Tuesday morning, so...two days." He checked his watch and frowned. "Did you dream?"

Two days? How could she have slept that long? She'd been known to sleep until nightfall on weekends after pulling an all-nighter at the bar, but still. She had to get back and check on the bar. Although the Knight Owl was closed on Mondays and Tuesdays, Emelia would have to call Renee right away to make sure everything went smoothly over the weekend. Renee wasn't a stranger to running the bar, and Emelia was grateful she had someone to call while she ran off to the city with Drake, but it was time to get back.

Drake's voice droned in her ears, fighting with odd, resurfacing memories from the gala. Hadn't there been fur and...snapping teeth?

She blinked quickly, realizing she hadn't answered his question. "I'm sorry, what?"

"Did you dream while you slept?"

"No, no dreams." She stroked her collarbone, remembering stabbing pains shooting through her neck. She pulled the collar aside and rubbed where she was sore. Nothing but pink, swollen flesh. Her right thigh was sore, too. Steading herself, Emelia glanced under the sheet. A light purple bruise marred her skin. Memories slapped her cold. The attack. The wolves. *Drake*. She forced herself to remain calm and get answers to the questions buzzing like bees in her brain. "Everything... really happened, didn't it?"

"Yes." Drake's lips fell into a grim line and he folded his arms across his chest. He looked like he was protecting himself from something...but that would be ludicrous, wouldn't it? What would he have to be afraid of in his own home?

"I'm sorry for what I had to do," he said. "But after what happened, there was no choice. You must have a million questions."

"The stranger from city hall..." Emelia swallowed hard. Drake handed her a second water bottle that she downed as quickly as the first. "He was your brother?"

Where did this insatiable thirst come from? And why was Drake acting like he knew what she'd want, before she wanted it?

"Unfortunately, you met my twin, Silas. I can't apologize enough for what happened. I'd meant to keep you out of all this and I sure as hell didn't expect him to attack you. Rest assured he'll pay with his life for what he did to you." He spoke with heated determination, each word gruff and clipped.

Emelia licked her cracked lips, then let her tongue settle on the jagged tip of her newest canine. "My teeth, they're—"

"Canines." Standing, Drake circled his chair and gripped its raised back. He looked weary and concerned. Like he wanted to put the chair between them for a reason. "Your teeth will change at first, but they'll go back to normal once you continue with your regular diet. They'll only elongate at the full moon after that."

"What are you saying?" Heat rose to her cheeks. "The full moon will...*what*?"

Now it was Drake who tensed. "My brother and I are werewolves, Emelia, born to werewolf parents. After Silas bit you, I had no choice but to bite your thigh and finish the process he'd started. If I'd left you the way I found you, you'd be dead. But now, because of the two bites, your body will"—he rolled his shoulders back and slapped a stoic, unreadable expression on his gorgeous face—"have the ability to shift into a werewolf as well."

"What the hell!" Emelia jumped out of bed so quickly, she dragged the blankets with her. "Werewolves? This isn't happening, I'm dreaming, that has to be it. This is a horrible dream brought on by the attack the other night. Right? Drake, tell me I'm having a nightmare."

Drake reached out for her. "I wish I could tell you that this is all a bad dream, but I can't."

"You've got to be fucking kidding me! Werewolves? In Seattle?" Her legs twitched, cramped, seizing with sharp knots of pain. She paced, stomping to shake the quivers out of her legs. "I'm a werewolf? Wonderful. I'm going to turn into a monster and howl at the full moon like the bloody, hairy mess in *American Werewolf in Paris* and shit. Oh God, your brother told me what would happen if he bit me. I saw…"

Drake in wolf form, fighting his brother…to protect her.

Drake tunneled his fingers through his dark mess of hair. "Yes."

"I saw you…as a wolf."

"I should apologize for scaring you that way, but what I did was absolutely necessary."

"You didn't scare me," she corrected, stopping in front of him. Drake's complexion had drained to ghastly white, as pale as the shirt pulling taut over his chiseled body. "I was never afraid of you."

The panic whirling inside Emelia died down as she stared into Drake's smoldering dark eyes. She became hyperaware of the heat radiating from his body. Of the magnetism pulling her body to his.

"Emelia, you're handling this really well," he said. "Most turned werewolves can barely hold on to a thread of sanity for the first few days."

"Believe me, Drake, I'm not handling any of this well." Emelia fought the urge to grab Drake by the waist and claw her fingers into his sides, raking her nails along the hard grooves of his abs…instead, she clutched the fabric over her stomach and gritted her teeth. She should be panic-dumb and tingly numb, not focusing on her arousal and how hot Drake looked. "I feel like I'm rotting away. My insides feel raw and worn, yet I feel like there's fire chugging through my veins. My arms are tight, and my legs ache like I'm having growing pains." What would she become when this was over? A wolf like Drake—one who is commanding, yet has an uncanny sense of calm about him? Or would she turn evil like his brother and become a wolf who kills for her own gain? "I don't feel right…I can feel myself changing. I don't want to become a monster."

"Just because you shift into a werewolf doesn't mean you'll start terrorizing small villages like in movies." He spoke tenderly, his voice warm with remorse. "We're more civilized that you'd believe."

"I don't know what to think." Cold from the inside out, Emelia shook her head. "Who the hell am I now?"

Drake cupped her chin in his massive hands. "You're Emelia Hudson, but your friends call you Emie. You love Château Lafite and hate costume parties. You curse like a sailor, have an unrivaled sense of pride when it comes to your bar, and are as stubborn as a mule. You're also the most beautiful woman I've seen in all my years on this earth. You're kindhearted and humble, showing compassion to every person who comes into contact with you. Beneath all that, you now have the molecular structure of a werewolf and will shift into one at every full moon. You're going to be fine and I'll be here to help you every step of the way."

Something in Emelia's chest fluttered, then caught. No matter what happened two nights ago, or two nights from now, Emelia knew she would be all right. An unnatural sense of calm inked through her, blanketing her frayed nerves. "How can this be real? Werewolves? Next you're going to tell me vampires are real, too."

"At least your sarcasm hasn't gone anywhere," he laughed, dropping his hands back to his sides. She wished his hands would return and stroke over the goose-bumpy skin beneath her shirt. "Vampires aren't real, at least not that I know of, though I suppose they could be in hiding like we are."

As the air charged with something electric, Emelia stepped back, then blew out a deep breath. It was the oddest thing…she could almost taste the energy sparking from Drake's body. It tasted exactly how he smelled—dark, spicy, and deliciously male.

Drake's dark eyes widened in hunger as if he understood what she sensed. "Your system will be on overload for the next few days. Senses and emotions will be heightened to extremes and fluctuate on whims. Impulses will be nearly impossible to control. Your inner thermostat will run freezing cold, then blistering hot."

"Basically, you're saying I'm like a computer that's about to crash: unreadable, unmanageable, freezing, then burning up."

The hard line of his lips quirked. "If you say so."

"Not that I'd know from working with Wilder Financial's computers or anything."

"Um-hmm."

Smelling the aroma of roasted garlic, succulent tomatoes, and buttery crust, Emelia's mouth watered and her gaze homed in on the bedroom door. Two short knocks pounded from the other side.

"Thank you, Raul," Drake said, striding to the door.

Taking care of business in his usual dominant manner, Drake rolled in a heaping cart of food, and stopped it near the table in the corner. Emelia hadn't noticed, but the bedroom wasn't really a bedroom at all. It was more like an elegant studio apartment with rich cherrywood furnishings, a partial kitchen—fully stocked, no doubt—and an open door that led to a gigantic bathroom.

"How many werewolves are out there?" Emelia asked, staring at the steaming pizza, her insides curling into one giant knot. She couldn't bear the thought of eating, though that was ridiculous, wasn't it? She was hungry, she had to be. She hadn't eaten in two days. Twenty minutes ago she'd wanted pizza, now…she couldn't pinpoint what she wanted.

Drake poured a glass of scotch from a bottle on the bottom rack and drank. "In the United States there are four hundred, and over a third of those belong to my pack."

"*Your* pack?" Her gaze shot from the stuffed crust to Drake.

"My father was an Alpha, and the ruling of the pack continues down generational lines."

Did he dominate everything in his life? "And your twin? Is he an Alpha, too?"

"Since we're twins, we're both technically Alphas by birthright. Catch the rub?" Drake sat on the leather sofa in front of the curtain-covered windows and leaned forward, stroking his thumb across the lip of the glass. "Our father was determined not to have his empire weakened by being split in half, so he decreed that the first son to find his Luminary would become Alpha and gain control over the pack, and the other son would take over the investments."

"What's a Luminary?" Emelia asked, taking the seat

next to Drake. His natural scent seemed to soothe the ache hollowing her middle. She couldn't be close enough.

"I think it might be best not to get overwhelmed in the details. Not yet, anyway. Right now we need to focus on easing your transition. Why don't you get something to eat? The entire cart is for you. There's breadsticks, soda, salad, pizza. I promised the best in the city."

Emelia felt her face crinkle. "I'm not hungry anymore."

"Craving flips are normal. If the pizza's no longer appealing, I can get you something else."

Emelia had never been cared for this way. Not before her parents kicked her out at eighteen for being too rebellious, and not when things had been good with Undercover Jackass, before he left her at the altar.

"Why are you being so nice to me?" she asked.

Drake's expression softened, and once again, Emelia glimpsed the kindhearted Oz behind the ironclad business facade. "If you don't eat, the transition will only get more difficult to handle. Your body needs fuel."

"No," she said, staring at the crisscross patterns in the rug. "It's more than the transition."

"You're a very special woman, Emelia." Drake set his empty glass on the floor and turned to her, sending waves of chills rolling through her body with a single glance. "If you weren't already spoken for, I'd show you just how special you are."

"I don't know what gave you the impression that I'm spoken for," Emelia said, "but believe me, on a scale of single to married, I'm beyond hopeless."

"Your Facebook relationship status says 'it's complicated,' so I assumed—"

"You checked my Facebook?" Emelia felt the first surge of anger like a lightning strike. It was harsh and hard-hitting, lancing through her temples. "You don't seem like the social media type."

"Trixie checked for me."

"I see."

"I also checked county records," he said. "You filed for a marriage certificate, but when you applied with the temp agency, you declared that your title was *Miss* Emelia Hudson." Drake's tone slipped into accusatory territory. Like she'd kept something from him that she should've revealed.

She didn't owe Drake an explanation of why the marriage didn't happen or why she'd chosen not to tell anyone at his company. Emelia couldn't explain why heat surged through her at the mention of her close-call marriage—maybe it was because she'd tried so hard to separate Jackass from anything involving Drake. Or maybe she was more irritable than normal. Whatever the reason, Emelia didn't care.

She didn't owe him anything, but she couldn't hold back.

"I filed for a marriage certificate because I'd planned on getting married," she spit out the words as if they were poison. "But that didn't happen when Mr. Jackass decided he'd rather run off into the sunset with one of the strippers at his bachelor party than marry me. He left me to face everyone the next day at the wedding, to tell everyone that my shattered dreams were his amusement, to stare into everyone's shocked faces. I wasn't the one who wanted a big wedding in the first place. I told him I wanted to elope, but it's not like he listened to anything I said anyway. I didn't change my Facebook because my life is fucking complicated all around, so I thought the tag was more fitting. And if I get asked about him again, someone might lose a head."

Drake sat in silence, gazing across the room as if he was lost in thought. The eruption of anger felt damned good. Emelia could breathe again. Think again. A weight had been lifted off her shoulders. Still, the tension clenching her stomach remained as intense as ever.

As Drake's gaze returned to her, Emelia could've sworn there were thoughts of murder brewing in it. "I'm sorry for what happened," he said, his hands clenched into fists at his side. "It'd be my pleasure to hunt down your ex-fiancé and bring him to you."

"If you hunt him down, kill him while you're at it," she said. "Why the hell would I want him brought to me?"

"You accepted a proposal of marriage. Where I come from, he is still yours."

"That's absurd." Emelia laughed, sensing something new emanating from Drake. It reeked of jealousy, knocking her anger off-kilter. "I don't love him anymore."

Drake stiffened at her words. "Then that's something different entirely."

There it came again—the scent of arousal blooming on the air, overpowering Emelia's other senses. She could almost taste Drake's pheromones. They flowed thick and rich into the air, calling her to come closer, coaxing her into submission. Her body responded to Drake on a primal level. Warm wetness pooled between her legs and her nipples hardened, waiting for his touch.

"What can I do?" Drake asked, his voice a velvety husk. "You won't eat and your temper flares are mild compared to others I've seen. You're taking the transition so much differently than other turned werewolves. I don't know what you need unless you tell me."

"I feel like I need…"

Crazy hot sex to drive away every last, irritating thought about her old life—the one where she was angry at the world for dealing her a sour hand.

"What?" he prodded, keeping his distance. "Tell me what you need."

"I need"—*something hard to pound away the ache*—"to feel."

As something inside Emelia cracked, she leaped on top of Drake and attacked him with her mouth and hands. Her lips crushed his. Her hands covered his body, neck to chest, to the ridge of his pants. The kiss was hot and intense, dizzying Emelia so much that Drake had to hold her in place with a firm hand against her back. He tasted like warm, buttery scotch and dark temptation. He was everywhere at once — clawing up her back, digging his hands through her hair, plunging his tongue in her mouth. It was sensory overload that drove Emelia to the brink of insanity.

Desperate to eliminate the space between them, Emelia straddled Drake's middle. Threw her head back and ground her hips against him. As the hard rod of his arousal pressed against her stomach, Emelia groaned and kissed him again. Harder. Deeper. Opened her mouth wide and explored the wet cave beyond his rich, supple lips. They melted together as Emelia raked her fingers through Drake's hair and pulled him against her, mashing his lips against hers. When she was finished with him, he wouldn't be able to pry her off with a crowbar.

Chapter Twelve

Molten heat surged through Drake's bloodstream, mixing with the blooming scent of Emelia's arousal and the honey-sweet taste of her mouth, creating a cocktail of passion that drugged him senseless. Her lips smothered his. Her tongue sank into his mouth. Tasting. Exploring. She'd always been a terrific kisser—it was all he could think about lately. But now something was different. She kissed him with unbridled passion. Like he wouldn't be able to stop her if he wanted to.

Stopping didn't cross his mind.

Throwing her head back, Emelia's waterfall of golden hair flipped behind her head and her chest arched forward. Drake palmed her milky-white breasts through the shirt, letting the heavy weight of them fill his hands. Two tiny pink nipples pressed against the thin fabric. Oh, they would taste as good as they felt, wouldn't they? He had to see her, and feel her, flesh against flesh.

"Get this off me," she ordered, bending down to assault his mouth once more.

She'd sensed exactly what he wanted. Couples usually

had to complete the Luminary bond before sensing each other's rising need…

Drake peeled the shirt over Emelia's shoulders and outstretched arms, leaving her in nothing but the black lace panties she'd worn beneath her gala dress. They barely separated their mouths to let the shirt pass between them, then attacked each other once more.

"Mmm," Emelia said, licking her lips as she writhed her hips against him. "You kiss different than you did before. You taste different, too."

"It's the transition."

Drake slid lower, smashing into the cushions, so that he was almost flat beneath her. Her breasts dangled in his face, perfect, soft, and begging to be suckled. Softly, he plucked one of her nipples between his fingers, then caught the other with his mouth. She moaned in response, her skin going flush beneath his tongue.

"Everything you feel will be heightened." He flicked a tightly budded nipple with his tongue, relishing the throaty moan that escaped Emelia's lips.

"It's like I'm waking up," she said, breathless. She splayed her legs wider over his lap. Until the heat from her center radiated through Drake's pants. "Like I'm feeling things for the first time. I can sense your hunger."

"I can feel yours, too. It's like a craving that's clawing its way through me." The words came out as a string of growls, rough and bumpy. He dragged his hands over her back and tugged on the ends of her hair. "I'll feed your hunger if you'll let me."

"Don't make me beg for it."

She caught Drake's lips and slanted her mouth to deepen the kiss, heating his body to dangerous levels. He wouldn't be able to hold out much longer. His erection throbbed fiercely, hardening to the point of pain. He kneaded her hips and guided them in a slow, grinding rhythm over his lap. The friction only increased his desire to push inside her.

"I've hungered for you since the first moment I saw you," he said as she arched up, rolling her hips over him like a skilled rider.

She was glorious above him, powerful and somehow majestic with her hair falling over her shoulders and her breasts gently bouncing in his face. Soft amber light from the candles on the dresser flickered over Emelia's tan skin, giving her a radiant glow.

He needed more taste, more feel, more of her hips grinding against him...without the clothes. As Drake possessed her mouth, Emelia ripped his shirt down the middle. Their mouths collided. Buttons flew. She jerked the shirt off his shoulders and groaned into him, leaning down until her breasts smashed against his chest.

Skin to flaming hot skin. *Finally.*

Drake quivered with the strength of his need. The raw seduction of her kiss. The way her body spoke to him in a way he'd never thought possible. His heart raced with hers. His breathing hitched with every one of her breathless moans. As warmth pooled between her legs, his shaft swelled and bucked, aching to feel her muscles clench around him.

Emelia was his.

He'd known it the second he touched her in the wine cellar. If it were up to him, and him alone, he would bond with Emelia, claim her as his Luminary, and welcome her like a queen into his pack.

Their lives would be linked. They'd never be apart. Damn the consequences.

But it wasn't only up to him. Emelia had a choice. Just because she was going to transition into a werewolf didn't mean she had to bond with him for the rest of her life. And most women wanted children, didn't they? How would she react when she found out that she would never be able to carry his child to full term?

One step at a time, he reminded himself. One step at a time.

"Emelia," he breathed.

"Yes?" She nipped at his earlobe.

"You have a choice in this."

She hesitated, propping her hands on the back of the couch on either side of his head.

"Oh, you want me to beg? Is that it?"

"No." *I want you to stay with me forever.* "I want you to know you have a choice."

"My choice is you." She smothered a kiss on his lips. "Right here." And another. Hotter. Deeper. "Right now. Take me, Drake." She stroked his shaft through his pants. "Take me before I burst."

A teasing spirit flittered through him. "Yes, ma'am."

Looping one of his arms behind her back, Drake grabbed hold of Emelia's waist and flipped her over in one swift move. She gasped as her head hit the couch cushions and her legs fell apart. Drake kneeled on the floor. Spread her legs apart farther and dove between them. Hooking a finger beneath her damp panties, he gave them a hard yank and tore them in two.

"Hope those weren't your favorite pair." He planted a kiss on her center and dragged his tongue through her wet slit.

"No." She blew out a ragged breath, and curled her hips to meet his mouth.

"I'm sorry," he said playfully, stopping to meet her heavy-lidded gaze. "Did you say something?"

He flicked her engorged nub with his tongue and watched her thighs tremble.

"Don't you dare stop." Grasping fistfuls of his hair, Emelia shoved his face back down into position.

No talking, then. Fine by him.

With a devious spark flaring inside him, Drake shot out his tongue and raked it across her flesh. She tasted better than he could've imagined—sugary sweet. Downright delicious. He teased her pleasure spot, biting and nipping. Responding to each of her body's subtle vibrations. As she began to tremble, Drake palmed her rear and lifted her hips against him. He slipped a finger inside her core, giving her the pressure she craved, while dragging his tongue through her slick folds. When her orgasm hit, she cried out his name and rocked against his mouth, driving him to the edge of his own release.

"You taste sweeter than wine," he said, wedging his hips between her legs. "I'm going to take you now."

Her kiss-plumped lips pulled into a smile. "Do you always make an announcement before you come?"

"In my pack, it's customary when the level of respect for your woman matches your desire." He planted an openmouthed kiss on her lips that buzzed through his chest. "I've only said those words to you."

"I see." Her smile widened, lighting the room. "Well? I'm waiting."

He kicked off his shoes and stripped out of his pants, all the while holding her gaze. As he settled his hips between hers once more, she sat upright and scooted to the very edge of the couch. She grasped his shaft, inhaling sharply when he twitched in her hand. Throbbing as every ounce of blood swelled him tighter than he'd ever been, Drake let his head fall back and his hips push forward.

"You're huge," she said, as she stroked him harder, clenching her fist around the long, thick length of him. "Are all werewolves—"

"No, baby," he interrupted, sweeping his fingers through her center. "Just me." He licked her succulent juices off his fingers and groaned. He pushed forward, until the head of his erection poised at her drenched core. "You're so wet. So perfect."

"Do you have protection?" she asked quietly, her chest heaving with labored breaths.

"No." Why would he carry around a condom? Diseases didn't pass from werewolves to humans, and she'd have to be a werewolf in heat to get pregnant. But he couldn't get into any of that. Not yet. "Do you?"

She nodded and pointed to the foot of the bed where her purse had been laid. "In the inside zipper pocket."

Drake fished through her purse and found the condom. "So tell me, sweet, innocent Emelia," he teased, tearing through the foil wrapper. "Were you planning to seduce me after the gala?"

With heavy-lidded eyes, Emelia watched as Drake put on the condom and approached her squirming legs. "I didn't think it'd hurt to be prepared."

"What a good girl you are."

As Drake wedged himself between Emelia's legs, his veins flooded with heat. She scooted closer to the edge of the couch and lay back, propping her head on the pillows behind her.

"Good?" she said, letting out a shallow hiss of air as the thick head of his erection brushed over her slit. "Don't you want me to be naughty?"

Holding on to a weakening thread of control, Drake maneuvered slowly, inching himself inside her. When he finally sheathed himself to the hilt, he groaned, clenching his teeth until he thought they would shatter. He had to go gently if he didn't want to hurt her, but it went against every pounding desire he had. Emelia groaned with him, moving her hips in a rhythm that stroked him from the inside out. She was so tight. A perfect fit.

"I want you," he mumbled, his jaw going rigid. "I want

you in every way."

As she began to writhe in her own rising pleasure, Drake reached out, splayed his hands over her stomach and massaged her breasts. He continued his path up her body, stroking his hands up her silky-smooth chest and looping them behind her neck. Gently, he grasped the back of her neck and tilted her head so that she could look in his eyes when he came. God, how he wished he could capture this moment. She was breathtaking. Glorious. Heart-stopping.

"Emie. My Emie." His voice strained hoarse. He was surprised he could speak at all. "Come for me again."

"Now?" she asked, pushing against the pillows, bucking against him. "You want it now?"

He was drawn so tight, his body clenched with raging need.

"I'm begging." Drake could feel her inner muscles begin to clench. He hardened into a giant knot, on the verge of climax. What scared him was the reaction that shot through him: the desperate urge to bond with her.

Drake clamped down the primal need, determined to give Emelia the choice first. Being with him physically, matching him like no other could, didn't mean she wanted to enter into the human equivalent of marriage with him.

"Come back," she breathed, her mouth falling open as she gasped for air.

Drake thrust into her harder. With all the force he had. "I didn't go anywhere. Come for me, baby."

With a resounding push, Emelia crumbled, her inner muscles flexing and releasing, pulsing as the orgasm milked its way through her. Drake continued to thrust, so achingly close to reaching his own jagged peak of release. The world shook before his eyes. Emelia sat up and kissed him, plunging her tongue into his mouth in time with his thrusts.

The pressure building inside Drake became too hot, too

great. He exploded, releasing his seed in deliciously sharp spasms that had him crying out her name.

Emelia was his woman. Bonded or not.

Chapter Thirteen

"You didn't have to do this all for me," Emelia said, staring at Drake from her stool across the granite island. "I could've eaten the pizza. It would've been fine."

They'd made love three times since she woke from her transition slumber, and while her cheeks had flushed a delicious shade of pink, her skin was paler than it'd been before. Emelia needed to eat a good, solid meal to rejuvenate her system. He would be damned to serve her cold pizza.

"I told you it's no problem." Drake stirred the tomato sauce and turned down the boiling water on the back burner. "I like to cook."

"You're sure you didn't come from a Good Husbands catalog or something?"

He gazed at her over his shoulder and watched wonder spark deep in her eyes. "They have such a thing?"

"No, I don't think so." She smiled, adjusting his T-shirt over her shoulders. "But if they did, I'm sure you'd grace the cover."

Drake couldn't ignore the pride whipping through him—

instead of dressing in the clothes Raul had picked up from Emelia's apartment, she'd chosen to slip back into his shirt. He dropped the spaghetti into the pot and focused on shoving them into the bubbling water so she wouldn't see the glow emanating from within him.

"Why don't you have a chef?" she asked.

"I tried that once," he said, precisely measuring out garlic, pepper, and Italian seasoning, then dumping them into the sauce. "But the one I hired cooked new-age health food that had no flavor. He insisted I eat healthier to elongate my life. He was an idiot."

The sauce began to bubble, so he clamped the lid down, poured a glass of wine, and handed it to Emelia. Would it always be this way if she became his Luminary and stayed by his side? They could make love all evening, steal down to the kitchen to cook up a midnight snack, then go back to bed and fuck until morning. Drake had given up the thought of bonding with someone—he'd grown accustomed to living on his own. But if Emelia stayed with him he wouldn't have to turn on the television over dinner to create noise so the house wouldn't feel as vacant. He wouldn't have to read in bed until he fell asleep so the night wouldn't seem so cavernous. Emelia would be there every step of the way with her spunky wit, effortless beauty, and challenging mind. It could be good, Drake realized. It could be great.

"That brings up a good point," she said. "How old are you?"

"How old do you think I am?" Drake sipped on his own wine as he stirred the noodles.

"Thirty?"

"Not far off." He shrugged. "I'm three hundred."

Emelia choked. "Three hundred years old?"

"Give or take a few decades."

"But wait, at the Vanguard Gala the host said Serephina

was born in the late eighteen hundreds. I'm no Einstein when it comes to math, but I think there's a missing century in there somewhere."

Drake leaned over the counter, amazed at Emelia's memory. "When we moved to San Francisco, my mother falsified her birth certificate so she could become more involved in the city council. If anybody dug around, they would find the truth."

"I see." Emelia sipped on her wine. "So at the ripe age of three hundred, are you an old or young wolf?"

"The average werewolf lives a thousand years. *If* they can find their life mate."

"Oh." Emelia's breathing slowed—Drake could sense it, hear it. "And if they don't find their mate?"

Drake went back to manning dinner. "A mateless werewolf will live maybe three-quarters of that, between six and eight hundred years. It's not an exact science. Some werewolves are stronger and heartier, so they'll naturally live longer than their weaker packmates. But my father believed that werewolves, like men, need women to balance and support them. He believed that men are weaker and incomplete without a woman at their side."

Emelia's arms suddenly slipped around Drake's waist. "I think your father is brilliant."

"He *was* brilliant," Drake corrected, leaning into her. "My father passed away some time ago."

Drake hadn't heard Emelia approach, but he breathed deep as she laid her head against his back and wrapped her arms tightly around his middle. He'd left his shirt upstairs and had dressed in nothing but plaid pajama pants that hung low on his waist. As Emelia's fingers slowly danced over his abs, teasing him with the promise of traipsing lower, Drake was glad he'd left his shirt upstairs.

Emelia went up on tiptoe and smudged a kiss on Drake's

shoulder, sending starbursts of shivers exploding down his spine. Fantasies of taking Emelia on the counter, the floor, the table, shot through his mind like comets.

"You're going to burn the sauce," she whispered.

"Damn it." The sauce had splattered on the lid and seeped onto the burner, making a giant mess. Part of Drake wanted to leave the spill, let the spaghetti burn, so that he could ravish Emelia again and again. How was it possible that she had become a welcome distraction in every part of his life, in just a few short weeks? "Let's eat."

They ate on the table poised between the kitchen and living room. Drake couldn't bear the royal-like formality of the dining room. Not with Emelia. It didn't feel right. It didn't…fit. He didn't want ten empty chairs between them as they sat on opposite heads of the table. He wanted Emelia close. Beside him. Where he could rub her thigh beneath the table between bites if the urge struck him.

Through dinner, Emelia had a million questions about the transition and what to expect, and Drake answered every one honestly, with as much clarity as he could. And every time he had the impulse to rub her thigh, he did. Although Emelia smiled and seemed to tremble at his touch, her sapphire eyes remained guarded. Even as she pulled her hand away, she hesitated as if removing her hand from his went against her deepest wishes.

What was holding her back from getting close to him outside of the bedroom? Could she not feel how deep their connection had rooted?

"Some of what happened at the gala is still a blur," Emelia said, finishing up the last of the spaghetti, "but I remember your brother saying something about ruling the pack."

Lost in thought, Drake clinked his fork against his plate. "Why would he mention that to you?"

"I think he said something about using me to get all of

it…the pack and the estate."

"Shit." Dropping his fork, Drake leaned back in his chair and folded his arms across his chest, as if he needed to brace himself against hurricane force gusts of wind. "He was going to hold you ransom for everything. Son of a bitch. He must've been the one to send that goon to attack you in the parking lot…I should never have underestimated him."

Emelia blanched. "Your brother sent that guy?"

"Not guy, Emelia. Werewolf."

"Shit is right." She guzzled her glass of wine and poured another.

"I should've told you, but I wanted to ease you into my world. I didn't even know if you'd want to be a part of it. Guess there's no choice anymore."

"Why me? I mean, why do I matter, anyway?" Emelia's neck flushed red, showing the signs of a pre-transition temper flare. "Why does your brother care who I am or bother sending some guy to attack me? Until two months ago, I was just a bartender. I'm nobody in your world."

"No, you're more than that." Drake took her hand and squeezed when she tried to pull away. Her skin was scorching hot. "There's something I haven't told you. Something I've been waiting to say until the right moment."

"You know, I'm barely on board with the werewolf thing. I'm already prepared to invest in Nair to take care of the nasty hair problem I'll have. Do you know how many hours it'd take to wax a wolf? I Googled it!" She nodded quickly, prompting him to answer, but left him no time to do so. "Like ten hours, Drake, ten! Now you're springing another surprise on me? If you say I'm gonna sprout three heads or become the next Godzilla, I might have you kill me now."

"You're my Luminary," he said, throat drying, heart drumming. "You're the one I'm destined to be with, the one who makes my life whole and complete. You're the one I've been waiting for my entire life. But the same thing that makes you my heart's greatest blessing makes you Silas's greatest threat. I guess I didn't realize how bad he wanted to be Alpha until now."

"Hold the phone." Emelia licked her lips slowly, her gaze homing in on the hard angles of Drake's face. "If you're with me, you get control over the whole pack? Like a private army, all to yourself?"

"There is something specific that has to happen for us to complete the Luminary bond, but basically…yes."

"Listen, Drake—"

"Wait," he said. "There's more."

"I don't think I can take much more."

He sighed, though the breath did little to release the tension hardening his body to stone. "As the new Alpha, it's expected that I have heirs to the throne, but a female turned werewolf has never survived giving birth when the father is an Alpha. Our young are too powerful, even in the womb. Only a pure-blooded born werewolf would be strong enough to live through the experience."

Emelia looked sick, holding her stomach as if the words soured her dinner.

"Let me get this straight. You're an Alpha, need heirs, and I'm your Luminary, the one who is supposed to give them to you, but since I wasn't born a werewolf, I won't survive the birth?"

"Right." He nodded. "And neither will the children."

"Holy mother, Drake! How can you expect me to be on board with all of this? I mean, last month I was fine. My life was fine. I mean, it sucked hard, but at least I could wrap my mind around what the hell was going on. This…*all* of this… it's too much."

Drake's greatest fear unfolded before his eyes. He could sense Emelia shutting down and clamming up. He should've waited to tell her about the issues with having children. He should've saved the bomb for when her feelings weren't so clouded by the mind-fuck of transition.

He tried to analyze his own feelings instead, but they were a jumbled mess of duty and honor and a pinching in his heart that smarted a lot like love. If being with Emelia meant that he would never have children, never have an heir, he'd have to be satisfied with that, and deal with the ramifications of the pack when they crossed that bridge. It was the only thing he could do.

But his decision wasn't the only one to consider.

If Emelia mated with another wolf, she could have children just fine. In essence, he was asking Emelia to choose between a future with him and a future with children. The thought made his gut clench into a solid rock. The only way he had a shot was if Emelia didn't want children to begin with.

"A month ago," he said softly, "when you looked into your future, did you see children?"

"I just thought of something else." Her hand went soft in his. "I'm not just Silas's ticket to everything, I'm yours. Is that why you've been being so nice to me lately? Because you want to use me to satisfy some power trip and become Alpha? Is that why you've been letting me drive your car, taking me out, and—ah shit, I let you take me to bed."

"Do you really think I've been using you so that I could take control over my pack?"

"I know I had a vision of who you were before I met you. The person I envisioned would've stopped at nothing to claim what he believed to be his. Two weeks ago, it wouldn't have surprised me to hear that you were going to use me to get ahead in some twisted family game." She closed her eyes and shook her head. What Drake wouldn't give to know what she was really thinking. "But now, I feel something different. I don't think you'd do something like that, but…hell, I haven't known you long enough to know how or why you do anything. This whole thing doesn't sit well with me. It doesn't...*feel* right."

"Think about it logically," Drake said. "If I wanted to use you against my brother, I would've bonded with you already and moved packmates around to different corners of Seattle. There would've been some commands ordered. There would've been massive pack movement the second I heard you were in danger."

"That easy, huh? Screw the woman, conquer the world? You know, like the line from that show?"

"I think you mean something else, but given the circumstances, the logic makes sense, doesn't it?"

"Nothing about this makes sense, so you can't expect me to rely on logic." She took her last bite of pasta and pushed the bowl aside. "Sometimes you have to follow your gut and go with what you feel, and if you don't know what your gut's telling you, you wait until you do. Don't you ever base a decision on feeling alone?"

As Drake thought back over every business deal he'd ever made, Emelia's smile flickered like a half-watted lightbulb. Every move he'd made had been based on facts, including the decision to keep Emelia's bar in his possession so he could invest in the area and ramp up business. He'd been right to keep the Knight Owl. When things settled down, she could run it. They would own it together. If profits didn't climb, they'd sell it. Simple.

"You even measured out the seasoning in this sauce like every speck counted," she said.

"It does count." He leaned forward, clasping his hands in front of him. "It all counts for something. Didn't you enjoy the spaghetti?"

"It was downright grubtastic, but you probably could've thrown the ingredients into a pan and it would've come out tasting the same."

He wasn't even going to ask Emelia what *grubtastic* meant. He assumed it was good since she'd all but licked her plate clean.

"If I'd made the sauce any other way, the spaghetti would've come out tasting completely different. I made the spaghetti from a recipe that had been passed down from my grandmother. It has to be exact, down to the pinch. That's what makes it great. That's what makes it special."

Leaning back, Emelia chewed over his words and eyed the leftover sauce on the plate.

"Everything in my life has to have order," he said. "Everything has to make sense. If it doesn't, how do I know it'll turn out right?"

"You don't, Drake," she said, swiveling around, placing both her hands on his lap. "That's the fun of it."

"If you won't listen to what I'm saying, and you won't trust my words"—he reached out, brushing back the hair that fell at her temple—"then what do you feel in here?" He touched her chest and held his hand there, feeling her heart thump wildly against his hand. "Do you honestly feel like the only reason I'm with you now is because I want to dominate my father's pack?"

"What you don't understand is that I don't know if I can trust what you're saying, but I don't think I can't trust my heart either." She looked at him then. Right through him. "It led me astray the last time I did."

There was only one thing left for him to do. He had to prove his intentions.

"Then for now, stay with me. Let me protect you until Silas is found. He'll continue to hunt you down until you make your final decision, but at least if you're under the protection of my pack, he won't be able to get to you as easily."

"Wait—what final decision?"

"Just because I've found you doesn't mean you're

automatically bound as my Luminary, Emelia. You have a choice in the matter, too. I want you to *want* to be with me for the next seven hundred years. I want you to be by my side because you want to honor and love me, not because our meeting was fated by the stars."

"Drake, I—"

"Let me finish." Drake grasped both of Emelia's hands in his. Electric currents shot up his arms and rattled through his chest. "If you want to complete the Luminary bond with me, tell me now and we can get started building a future together, but that future won't involve children. If that's not what you want—if *I'm* not what you want—I give you my word that I'll continue to protect you. I'll ease you through the transition process, welcome you into my pack, and once Silas is gone and the threat to your safety is over, I'll make sure you're settled back in the routine of your normal life in the city. But I swear to you, here and now, no matter what you choose, I'll never bond with another."

Her perfectly arched brows rose as she worried her bottom lip between her teeth. "But you said your life would be shortened if you didn't bond with someone."

Drake couldn't hold back, not now. Not when the pressure in his chest was this tight. "If I knew I was never going to see you again, I'd choose to die tonight, with the taste of you still on my tongue, the feel of your body still on my hands, and your scent lingering in my nose, than live another day without those things."

Emelia threw back her chair and leaped into Drake's lap. He caught her, coiling his arms around her back, and brought her closer as she nuzzled into his neck. He'd waited so long for this moment—since he was first taught about Luminaries and soul mates and the completion of two lonely hearts. He'd been waiting for Emelia his entire damn life. There was no way he could've fathomed how empty his life was until this moment, when his heart felt so full it was liable to burst.

"Is this a yes?" he asked, allowing a sliver of hope to streak through him. Maybe the children issue wasn't an issue after all...

She planted fevered kisses on his neck, the underside of his jaw, his lips. Then Emelia laid her head against his chest and shook her head.

Confusion prickled the hairs on the back of Drake's neck. "No, then?"

"I don't know," she said, wiggling around so that she straddled his lap. "No one has ever talked to me the way you do. No one has ever made me feel this way, but—"

"But?"

"You can't expect me to make a decision this quickly. I mean, I love what's happening between us. I've never felt anything like this before." Her fingers danced across his chest in tiny swirls, chilling him with each gentle stroke. "I can barely keep my hands off you and I'd be stupid if I said I didn't dream of some knight in shining armor sweeping me off my feet the way you have. But after what I've gone through—first with my ex, then with all...*this*—I don't feel like it'd be a good move to jump into another relationship until I have my feet on solid ground. Not to mention the fact that I'm not sure if I want to scratch children off my list of possibilities yet. Bottom line, it's too soon, and you're asking too much. I don't really know you, and you don't really know me."

"No?"

"No." She kissed him softly, promising the world, but giving away nothing. "I feel like I need some time."

As Drake felt the cold grip of reality wrench his heart, he clenched his jaw until he thought the bone would break. Emelia's decision made sense. It was reasonable to take some time, given the circumstances. It was undeniably the logical thing to do. Despite how her words appealed to Drake's analytical side, the sting burned anyway, scorching through his chest.

Not knowing what else to do, Drake took Emelia's hand and softly kissed the delicate arch of her knuckles. "Take all the time you need."

Chapter Fourteen

At first, when Emelia turned down Drake's offer to be his Luminary, she thought she'd made a mistake. He was gorgeous, their chemistry was off the charts, he was stable and commanding, the take-charge kind of man she'd always dreamed of marrying. He made her heart race and her skin flush with a single glance. He would be able to take care of her like no other man could, especially now that she was changing into a werewolf.

The concept that she would shift into a werewolf at the full moon struck Emelia as ridiculous even now, though she couldn't deny the freakish changes happening to her body; one second she was sweating and pissed off, the next second she was cold as ice and laughing hysterically. It was mania at its best.

But Emelia simply couldn't answer Drake the way he'd wanted her to. He may not have been the devious man she'd believed him to be a month ago, but there was still so much she didn't know. She'd jumped into a relationship before, and it'd gotten her nothing but a broken heart, an unused wedding dress, and a bunch of gifts she didn't want and still had to return.

To top it off, Drake wasn't only asking her to be with him forever, he was asking her to drop her dreams of having children. Emelia hadn't even thought that far yet. She'd been so focused on building a thriving business with her bar, she hadn't had time to think through what would happen after that. Sure, children might've been in the picture someday, but not anytime soon. Did that mean she wanted to forgo that option completely?

No matter how badly Emelia wanted to say yes to Drake's offer, no matter how much her heart pulled to his, she couldn't accept.

Drake had dropped Emelia off at the Knight Owl bright and early Wednesday morning so she could catch up on paperwork and check on the weekend sales. Although she'd insisted that she would be all right by herself, Drake left three *packmates* with her—she would never get used to that word—while he left to handle business of his own.

Emelia pulled chairs down from the tabletops and shimmied them into place, adding tiny pumpkin-spice tea lights to the center of the tables to add a festive feel. There was a rainstorm coming, and Thanksgiving was around the corner. Customers would want to frequent a place where they could order an Autumn Tumbler, kick their feet up on one of the tables, and watch their favorite football team play on one of the flat screens mounted by the stage. Other customers would want to curl up with one of the books on the shelves in the back and put the worries of the day behind them.

That is, if customers would come in at all.

Emelia had always been good at knowing what customers wanted and what they needed in their local watering hole before they asked for it. She knew when they wanted stand-up comics and got them. She knew when they wanted open mic night and had arranged to have it on the first weekend of every month. Business went from trickling to booming in no time. Emelia had finally found something she was good at—running and maintaining her tiny sliver of heaven.

But over the last couple months, business had slowed to a halt, and it seemed that nothing Emelia tried brought customers back. It had to be the economy. Or maybe she'd slipped on paying attention to the customers' needs.

"Where are you going?" one of the guards asked as she walked around the wall separating the main room from the bar.

"To my office." She didn't stop walking, and became hyperaware that the guard shadowed her every step. "Is that a problem?"

"We were told to have you in sight at all times." He was the burliest of the three, with a skull-trim cut and dark, blazing eyes. "Direct order from Mr. Wilder, ma'am."

"Watch me at all times, huh?" Emelia swept past the bar and walked to her office tucked in the back near the kitchen. "And if I have to use the restroom? What then? You gonna follow me in and hand me paper?"

The guard flustered, clearing his throat. "I think, ah, I think it'd be best if you… Logan, it's your turn to guard the Luminary!"

Oh, wonderful. They all knew she was Drake's match. Did Drake tell everyone in the pack, or was their connection something they all sensed, like Silas?

Rolling her eyes, Emelia entered her office and plopped into the leather seat in front of her computer. "Friday was slow, Saturday was horrible," Emelia read aloud from a Post-it stuck to her computer screen. "Missed you. Hope you had fun in SF. Renee."

Emelia sighed, running her fingers through her hair. When she'd first approached Drake about the bar, when she still thought she owned it, he'd said the neighborhood was in a downward spiral. He'd said she would go bankrupt without serious financial backing. Damn him if he was right. Emelia couldn't deny that business was slower than normal, but customers came in waves. They would come back, wouldn't they? What if business never picked back up? And what the hell was she going to do about Needles and the money she had apparently flushed down the toilet?

She wished she had something saved up to hire a lawyer and sue the hell out of Needles and get her fifty grand back so she could reinvest in the bar. But damn it, there was nothing she could do. Drake owned her building. She'd have to go back to leasing it.

Like an elephant in the room that she refused to acknowledge, Emelia did everything she could not to think about Drake's offer. She couldn't push it aside any longer…if she married Drake, what was his would become hers.

She would own the bar again.

"No," she said aloud, plopping her head in her hands. "I bought it myself, built it up myself, and I'll do it again. I don't need anyone."

Emelia's heart sank, but it wasn't because she didn't know what she was going to do with her bar and Drake's building. Deep down, a tiny inkling warned that while she might not *need* anyone, she was starting to *want* someone by her side. And not just any someone, but one very special someone in particular.

Drake.

"What am I thinking?" She mindlessly stroked her left ring finger. "Things shouldn't be this difficult. What the hell am I doing?"

"If you've managed to keep this place up and running while everything around the neighborhood is falling apart," a scratchy voice said from the doorway, "I say you know exactly what you're doing."

The packmate leaning against the doorframe was smaller than the other two wandering around the bar, but he was still a whopping six-feet-something huge, with a mop of unruly black hair and enormous, piercing gray eyes. He was dressed in black leather pants, a baggy black shirt, and had the jaw-dropping good looks to grace the cover of *Muscle* magazine. But he didn't look plastic, like he'd gotten his build from the gym alone. No, he looked like a linebacker, rough and ready to do some real damage.

"Logan, I presume?" Emelia asked, scanning through the weekend's numbers. "Have you come to put me in my place?"

"No, ma'am," he said, folding his arms over his chest. "I came to serve you. What can I do?"

Hmm. This werewolf was different. Instead of picking up a warm, protective vibe from Logan, Emelia sensed an aloof type of coldness about him. Like pushing everyone away was his usual MO.

"Nothing," she said, lost in a document detailing profits and losses. "I'm used to handling everything on my own, but thanks for the offer."

"My pleasure. If you need me, I'll be manning the front door." As Logan retreated into the bar, Emelia called him back.

"There is one thing," she said, swiveling her chair around to him.

"Anything."

"Do you know Drake—Mr. Wilder very well?"

"Yes, ma'am," Logan said, with a quick, marine-like nod. "I owe him my life."

"How's that?"

Logan shifted his feet as if what he was about to say made him uncomfortable. "He set up a part of the Vanguard Foundation to take care of werewolves who are left parentless.

I was abandoned by my parents, who wanted to roam the world without a child hooked to their hip. I was left on the streets for years and had to fend for myself." He spoke as if the past were distant to him, a detached piece of his soul that floated around his body. "Turned werewolves only shift on the full moon, but born werewolves like me turn when they get angry. When you're left on the streets, nothing angers you more than having to fight for food. Until someone helps you control your anger, you get into heaps of trouble. Mr. Wilder was the one who helped me."

"Oh." It seemed like a stupid thing to say after what he'd just told her, but Emelia couldn't think of another word to take its place. The more she learned about Drake, the more he amazed her. She was terribly wrong on her first judgment. Drake wasn't evil. He was kind. Generous and loving. And for reasons Emelia still didn't understand, he *cared* for her. "How long have you known him?"

Logan couldn't have been more than thirty.

"Two hundred years, ma'am, and I can't say I've met a better man since then." Logan stepped into the room and took to a knee so that his steel-gray eyes were level with Emelia's. "If you don't mind my saying so, I heard what happened with Silas. I should say I'm sorry you were transitioned that way, but I truly think it's for the better."

Emelia sighed. "Yeah, well, there's nothing I can do about it now, even if I wanted to."

"Not that my opinion matters, but you should complete the bond with Mr. Wilder."

"Not that your opinion matters," she joked.

"Right." He nodded slowly as a smile teased the corners of his mouth. "I can sense your connection to him, and I can sense your apprehension. But I can sense more stirring within you, too. You're powerful, Ms. Hudson. You're graceful and unique, so much more than you believe yourself to be. You'd be a perfect match for him."

"Me? Graceful?" Emelia laughed, and felt for the first time like she had a friend in Drake's world. "Guess you haven't seen my feet get tangled together yet."

Logan matched her laugh, easing the tension in her middle. "You're very special, Ms. Hudson."

"I don't think she needs to hear that from you."

Emelia hadn't noticed Drake walk up behind him. Either the dimly lit bar cloaked Drake in shadow, or he moved with deadly stealth.

"Mr. Wilder," Logan said, standing, pulling his shoulders back.

"Mr. Black." Drake's words melted together into a growl.

"I was just asking Ms. Hudson if there was anything she needed."

"Bet you were."

The two faced off, toe-to-toe, and the next few seconds were taut with silence. If glares shot daggers in the literal sense, they would've been skewered through.

"What are you doing here, Drake?" Emelia shut down her computer and stood, smoothing down her jeans. "I thought you had business to take care of."

"I did," Drake said, not taking his eyes off Logan. Their gazes remained locked like ram horns in a brutal clash. "Emelia, may I speak to you in private?"

Logan nodded as if the question were meant for him, and left the office. "Nice to meet you, Ms. Hudson," he said without looking back.

"You too." Emelia pointed to the spot where Logan stood moments before. "What was that about?"

"I don't like him talking to you that way." He snaked an arm around Emelia's waist and tugged her against him. His belt ground into her stomach, then seemed to disappear as something harder swelled between them. "I've missed you."

"Is that what you came back to tell me?"

"That'd be sweet, but no." He smiled. "I came back to tell you that I found a lawyer who'll take your case against Mr. Branch."

"Really?" Emelia nearly jumped out of her skin, then steeled herself. "Thank you for setting that up, but I don't think I can afford a lawyer just yet."

He brushed his hands up and down her arms. "I'm taking care of it."

"No, no, that's not what I want." The last thing Emelia wanted was for Drake to think she was using him, or getting closer to him because of what he could do for her and this place. "When I can afford it, I'll hire a lawyer myself."

"I figured you'd say that," he said, stroking his hands over the small of her back, "so I found a lawyer who'll work the case pro bono. He's done a few cases with Wilder Financial, but he works for a separate legal corporation so you won't have to go through me or my company, if you don't want to. He said the case sounds clear-cut, but he'll take a deeper look once you give him the go-ahead. I put his business card on the bar."

"Thank you." Emelia couldn't believe Drake had gone out of his way to make her feel more comfortable with the situation. He'd made her next move clear…and convenient. "I'll give him a call this afternoon."

"I also came back for something else."

"Yeah?"

"I'd like to take you on our first date."

"Our first…*date*?"

"You know, where you get dressed up and I pick you up at your place and we go out to dinner and a movie like normal people?"

She smacked him. He didn't flinch, damn him and his brute strength. "I know what a date is, Captain Obvious. It's just that…aren't we past that? I mean, the dog has already buried the bone. What good would it do to dig it back up and show it to me?"

Deep hoots of laughter erupted out of him. "Yes, Emelia, I've already *buried the bone,* but if you wouldn't mind, I'd like to show you what it would be like to go out with me under normal circumstances. I'd like to show you what your life could be like if you stayed with me."

"Tempting offer," she said, plinking her fingers across her desk. "But I'm not sure."

"Damn it, woman, are you sure about anything?"

Her gaze drifted over Drake's shoulder, to the dartboard on the far wall. "Tell you what. We'll play a game of darts over it. If you win, I go out with you, wherever and whenever you want. If I win, you have to jump into Lake Washington."

"What? Why the hell would you want me to do that? The water's freezing!"

"Exactly the point," she said, smiling. "Jumping in defies logic."

He needed a lot more feeling and a lot less thinking in his life. If she had to be the person to show him what a little spontaneity was like, so be it. Besides, she'd jumped into Lake Washington dozens of times. The water wasn't *that* cold.

"It'll take an act of God to get me in there," he said.

"Or a losing game of darts."

"Yeah, that's not happening," he chuckled. "I've had hundreds of years to perfect my shot."

"Then you have nothing to worry about," Emelia said.

She held out her hand to seal the deal. Drake took it and shook, enveloping her hand in warmth.

"I tried to warn you, but if you insist on making this easy on me, lead the way." He swept his arm aside so she could pass through to the bar. "I'm thinking a steak and lobster dinner. Maybe a late-night jaunt to Victoria Island."

Emelia yanked six darts—three flagged blue, three flagged red—out of the cork board and turned. Drake stood on the throw line, gearing up to throw an invisible dart. Watching him lose was going to be the highlight of the night.

"You know, Drake," Emelia said, handing him the blue darts. "I just realized that I am sure about one thing."

"What's that?"

Smiling ear to ear, Emelia took her spot on the line and fired the first dart straight into the bull's-eye. "I'm gonna kick your ass."

Chapter Fifteen

"Tell me again what this proves?" Drake stood at the end of his pier that jutted into Lake Washington, and peered into the dark water.

"It proves that you're a man of your word. You lost that game fair and square."

Kneeling on the slated wood, Drake untied his shoes, slipped them off, then pushed them aside. "You could've mentioned that you were a ringer."

Emelia laughed. "You could've asked."

"I think you cheated." Moving as slow as molasses, Drake took off his coat, folded it, and draped it over his shoes. "Nobody gets three bull's-eyes from their first three shots."

"Nobody but a woman who has played in dart tournaments since she was sixteen." Emelia looked back down the long stretch of pier to where Drake's mansion perched on the raised bank, its warm lights beckoning them in from the cold. His home looked different than it did the night of the Halloween party. It looked warm. Homey and inviting. She wished she'd grabbed a blanket before heading down to the lake. Her raincoat and jeans did little to block the wind. "Come on, fishy-fishy, get swimming. It's freezing out here."

"My coat's right there. If you're cold, put it on." He stripped out of his shirt, robbing the breath from Emelia's lungs. The bright light of the nearly full moon gave Drake's chiseled body a glow that rivaled bronze statues. His muscles twitched and flexed as he unzipped his pants and yanked them down, then stepped out of them. "This is madness. I can't believe I'm doing this."

"It'll be over before you know it." Emelia brushed her hands over her arms and jumped up and down for warmth. "You can't think, you've just gotta jump."

Thunder rumbled overhead as drizzles of rain seeped from the night sky.

"Oh, sure, add some rain to the mix." Drake stepped out of his underwear and chucked them onto his pile of clothes, then stood at the end of the pier, hesitating. "You and Mother Nature must be in cahoots."

Emelia would've laughed at how big of a chicken Drake was being, but she couldn't clamp her mouth shut. His shoulders were wet, dripping with rain. Shadows played over his body, accenting the hard lines of his back, his rear. He was the most gorgeous guy she'd ever seen, a man who radiated power and dominance…yet he was scared of a little rain and a lot of water. He curled his toes over the edge of the pier and peered into the lake.

"Go," she whispered, losing her voice. Oh, how she wanted to sneak up behind him and rub her hands over the slick, pulsing muscles on his back. Okay, okay, so she wanted to shove him in. "Go!"

As lightning split the sky, Drake blew out a few quick breaths of air and jumped. He landed in the water with a giant splash and disappeared into the lake's murk.

Surprised he actually did it, Emelia ran to the edge. Drake

popped out of the water like a rocket, his eyes as wide and bright as silver dollars. "It's fucking cold!"

"It's November! Of course it's cold!"

"Ah shit, it's cold, it's cold, it's fucking cold!" He swam frantically for the ladder, his arms and legs flailing like he couldn't gain control of them.

She'd never seen his wall of composure crumble like this. It tickled Emelia down to her toes. She laughed, then felt bad, and met him at the ladder.

"Here, give me a hand," Drake said, stopping at the bottom. "Some of these steps are broken."

"See, that wasn't so bad, was it?" She teased, extending her hand.

Drake snatched her arm and yanked her into the water behind him, then toppled over with her. Emelia screamed as the water cocooned around her, sucking the air from her lungs. The frigid water burned on contact, prickling her skin with thousands of needles. Drake's legs tangled in hers, his arms lifted her up, and moments later they both emerged from the water gasping for air.

"You sucker!" she screamed, splashing Drake. "The water's freezing!"

He laughed. Really laughed. Then splashed her back.

Every muscle in Emelia's body went numb as something in her middle came to life. She buzzed with excitement and her heart swelled as she cowered from Drake's splashing assault. She swam away and kicked hard, drenching him with the force of her flapping feet. For the first time, Drake wasn't a shrewd businessman, her boss, or even a werewolf. She wasn't a bartender, or a secretary. Drake was her equal. A man who made her feel like no other could. Emelia was freezing, her extremities going numb, her mind screaming at her to get out of the water as fast as she could. But there was nowhere else she wanted to be.

Drake swam toward the ladder and tugged Emelia along. She laughed between gasping breaths and didn't miss each opportunity to splash Drake in the back.

"Come on, let's get out of here," he said, holding on to the side of the ladder. Rain fell on his lashes, drenching his face. "You first."

Emelia took the first submerged step, felt Drake's leg brush hers, then stopped when an electric current surged between them.

"What are you waiting for?" he said, as rain fell harder, dimpling the water around them.

As Emelia's heart leaped, she said, "This," and pressed forward, catching his mouth. His lips were slippery and soft, sliding against hers in an erotic dance that she didn't want to end. His tongue caressed hers with dizzying skill, reminding Emelia of Drake's unmatched talent in the bedroom. He moaned into her, sliding his arms around her waist as if her figure had been molded to fit perfectly into his embrace. With a firm hand against Emelia's hip, Drake guided her to the stairs, so that her back was flush against them. He pinned her there, wedging his thigh between her legs, and continued his possession of her body. She gasped for air, clutched at his back, and ached to taste more of his lips.

He dove down to her neck, smudging deliciously wet kisses along her collarbone, and back up to her chin. She quivered as his tongue shot out, tracing the tiny, circular indentation at the base of her neck. She lost her breath when his kisses turned to gentle sucks. And as Drake found her breasts beneath the water and massaged them in his strong hands, Emelia couldn't help but lay her head back and let the sensations flood her.

Between the frigid water lapping around them, the heat of Drake's mouth on her skin, and the warm rain falling on her face, Emelia could've exploded from sensory overload. His touch was electric, lighting her skin on fire. Her body responded instinctively by arching into him, begging to give him what he wanted. Despite the temperature of the water, she was warm with Drake's body crushing hers.

"You were right," Drake said, then continued to devour her mouth.

Emelia gasped for air, relishing the roughness of his hands as they raked over her body. "About what?"

"Everything," he said. Rain slid between their mouths, but couldn't quench Emelia's burning desire for Drake's body to cover hers. "If this is what I get for feeling instead of thinking, I think I should try it more often. Minus the midnight swim, of course."

Emelia smiled into another kiss, and as Drake effortlessly lifted her out of the water and set her on the pier, she laughed. He made her giddy. The way he eyed her body like it was his. The way he claimed and possessed her.

She couldn't get enough, and she knew she'd never tire of it.

As Drake emerged from the water, he swept Emelia into his arms and carried her to the opposite side of the pier, where a massive tri-level yacht was moored. The top decks were pearly white, with tons of windows and an open bow, while the bottom half was painted a glossy shade of midnight blue.

"Watch your step," Drake whispered, setting her down.

"What's up there?" Emelia's teeth chattered, and although she couldn't see her lips, she'd bet they were turning purple.

"I keep towels on the deck," he said, crossing his arms in a shiver. "Unless you'd rather run back to the house."

Running a few hundred yards in the pouring rain in soggy shoes didn't sound appealing.

"No, this is…fine." Her gaze trailed across the long, swooping deck of the yacht, then focused on the white, bulky letters stenciled on the bow: *Tara*. "A former flame?" she asked.

"Excuse me?" He took her hand.

"The name of the boat. Was Tara a former lover?"

Even through the pouring rain, Emelia could see hints of laughter sparkling deep in Drake's chocolate-toned eyes. "Tara is the name of the plantation in *Gone with the Wind*."

"You're a fan of the movie?" Emelia couldn't picture it.

"I'm more of an all-around classic movie fan. Back then, the men were smooth and the women had tenacity to spare. Doesn't get better than that." His full lips pulled into a smile and he squeezed her hand. "Now up you go, my lady." Holding her hand, Drake helped Emelia on board, then followed closely behind her.

The yacht was magnificent, long and sleek, with a formidable bow and bench seats lining the cabin. Although the boat was dark and quiet, bobbing smoothly on the water, Emelia bet the thing was powerful at sea—a beast. She stepped beneath a balcony to get protection from the rain. As if the storm knew the second she'd found somewhere dry, the rain began to fall harder, dripping from the edges of the awning like a lightly streaming waterfall. Drake popped the lid on a bench on the deck as Emelia breathed deep. How had she ended up on the most luxurious yacht she'd ever seen, on Lake Washington, in the middle of a rainstorm, with the elusive Drake Wilder? Two months ago she wouldn't have believed she'd be here.

"Here." He draped a towel around her shoulders, then pulled her against him.

Emelia's body responded to Drake's body, not the terry cloth, and instantly warmed.

"Better?" he asked, pulling back to look into her eyes. "Your lips aren't so purple."

"Thank you." Lifting up on tiptoe, Emelia kissed him

with all the passion she'd kept buried inside. She tried to snapshot this moment—the sound of the rain, the way her stomach somersaulted when his tongue slipped inside her mouth. She wanted to keep this memory with her always. It was dreamlike. Beyond surreal.

Emelia's heart pinched as realization struck her like a thunderclap. This wasn't her reality...it might as well have been a dream. Drake wanted to show her what it would be like if she lived with him day and in and day out. If this was the life Drake wanted her to see—jet-setting to galas in the city, mansions in Seattle and San Francisco, and spending the night on an elegant yacht—she didn't fit. She was a middle-class, hardworking bartender. She couldn't talk to his associates the way he did. She couldn't drive his Mercedes every day, though she'd started to get used to how that car could get up and go.

How long would it take before Drake realized she didn't belong in his world?

As Emelia put her head on Drake's chest and scanned the long length of the yacht, she realized she was out of her league. If this was the way Drake lived, she'd never live up to it. She refused to live her life feeling inferior to what Drake had to offer. If they were going to be "bonded"—as he put it—she would need to feel like Drake's match.

If Emelia said yes to Drake, would she be marrying the businessman, or the carefree man who flapped around buck-naked in the lake? Would she be marrying the stern, unshakable man who loved extravagances that she couldn't dream of having, or the man she met in the wine cellar when he could've been the janitor or company security? If she was going to consider spending her life with him, Emelia needed more reality and less of...*this*.

An idea struck.

"I think I'd like to let you take me on that date," she said, as lightning lit the sky.

Would Drake continue to try to impress her with glitz and glamor or would he be the man she wanted him to be?

"I have some last-minute business to take care of tomorrow," he said, "but how does Friday night sound?"

"I have to work the bar on Friday."

"After your shift then?" He didn't skip a beat.

What kind of date starts at two in the morning?

"Okay," she said, struggling to remember that the date would have to happen on his terms. "Friday night sounds perfect." As a light on his neighbor's back porch clicked on, Emelia smiled. "I think your neighbors might be peeping on us."

"Only if they have a telescopic lens." Craning his neck around, Drake peered through the rain. Without warning, he hauled Emelia against him and bent her back into a dance-like dip. "If they're watching, let's give them the show of their lives."

Emelia's body surged with heat as Drake possessed her mouth and dragged her to the floor.

Chapter Sixteen

Early Friday morning, Raul pushed through the glass door leading to the conference room and took the seat across from Drake. The table was black and glossy, reflecting the blue of Raul's tie like a streak of lightning across a starless sky.

"Sorry I'm late, sir," Raul said. It looked like stress lines had been permanently etched into his face. "I have news on Silas."

They had assigned packmates to trail Silas since the night of the gala, but hadn't heard back. Silas had fled to the airport, where he'd had a private jet on standby. Where he'd taken off to was anyone's guess.

One thing Drake knew for certain: until Emelia became his Luminary she was still in Silas's sights. Killing Emelia before Drake bonded with her would be easy for Silas. There would be no one to answer to but Drake, and little consequence among their pack. Attacking Emelia after they bonded, however, would be a declaration of war. Silas would be seen as threatening their Alpha's woman, and that wouldn't be tolerated. If Silas attacked Emelia after they bonded, it'd be suicide.

"And?" Drake asked.

"We tracked Silas's plane to Colorado yesterday afternoon. Twenty packmates disembarked, including Silas. They boarded another private plane, flew north over the Canadian border, then veered west."

"They knew we were tailing them," Drake said, his insides coiling tighter and tighter.

"Yes, sir." Raul leaned back in his chair and tapped his pen nervously against the table. "They landed in Vancouver early this morning, then split up to confuse us. Half of his group boarded one plane and departed for London with a final destination of Greece. The other half boarded a second plane that didn't have a flight plan recorded. We have men stationed in Vancouver questioning traffic controllers for possible intel."

"Damn it." Drake's insides flared with anger. Clenching his fists, Drake stood and paced in front of the wall made of windows. The sky was smothered with gray clouds that drenched the city in dreary blurs of rain. "Which plane did Silas board?"

Raul shook his head slowly and swallowed hard. "One of our packmates claimed to see Silas board the Greece-bound plane, but upon further questioning, his certainty wavered."

"Damn it, Raul!" Drake spun around, his teeth chattering with pent-up rage. The wolf inside him rattled his bones, threatening to burst free. "That's not good enough! I want Silas found and I want him found now!"

Windows shook. The floor vibrated. They were nothing compared to the shock waves rolling through Drake's middle. He wanted Silas to pay with blood for attacking Emelia.

"Until Emelia makes her decision, she's in danger, Raul." Drake spat the words. "Alert the entire pack."

"Our best packmates are guarding her now, another two

are stationed outside her apartment, and the others in the area have been informed to keep an eye out for suspicious werewolf activity from neighboring packs."

"Good." Drake's mind raced. "It's nearly eight. Is everything ready?"

Silas had demanded a conference call with Drake at eight sharp. Drake had wanted to tell his brother to fuck off. That trying to kill Emelia might not have been a declaration of war, but it didn't matter—Silas had crossed the crazy line. But Drake couldn't pass up an opportunity to get a read on where Silas might be. He was probably calling midflight, but the sound of a mumbling packmate in the background or the slip of a pilot announcing their destination might be all it would take to reveal his location. He was looking for something. Anything.

"Everything's set," Raul said. "All our bases are covered."

"Damn well they better be."

Drake glanced at the wall to this right, the one filled with six very blank flat-screen televisions. The instant the clock ticked over to 8:00 a.m., the large screen in the center of the wall flickered to life. Silas's head and shoulders crowded the screen, making Drake feel like he was looking in the bathroom mirror. While Silas's hair was the same color as Drake's, dark like an oil slick, it was a bit shorter and didn't reach his ears. His jaw was just as square as Drake's, his brows just as thick, his shoulders just as broad. Only the tiny indention on Drake's left ear marked a difference between the twins, and most people never noticed.

"Brother," Silas greeted with a slippery smile. "Good to see you."

"Wish I could say the same."

Silas's smile dropped. "Down to business already? I haven't seen you in years and you can't find a 'howdy, brother' in you anywhere? Pity."

"You attacked an innocent woman. You think I'm going to kiss your ass and play nice simply because we share the same genes? Wouldn't count on it."

"Oh, she's far from innocent," Silas said, his dark eyes shadowing over. "We both know what she is. I felt your connection to her the instant you did."

"I want you to leave Emelia out of this." The fire in Drake's gut kindled with hatred. "How could you stoop so low, brother? How could you do it?"

They'd been close growing up, more than friends, more than brothers. They'd been inseparable. All it took was one fateful night, and one horrible mistake, for everything to flip on its head. Silas hadn't been the same since their father died. Since the night Drake was on guard and their father was attacked by an insane packmate who'd gone rogue. There was nothing Drake could've done to save their father. By the time the alert had been sounded, it was too late. But that didn't mean Silas forgave him for it. In fact, it was the unfortunate opposite. Silas hadn't stopped blaming Drake since the day it happened.

"I think you've forgotten that the position of Alpha was rightfully mine." Silas's eyebrows pinched. "You shouldn't be in this position. I was born first. If our father was alive, he would've been out of his prime. He would've passed the title to me, and you'd be waiting until he died to claim the investments in his estate."

"Father's death was not my fault, Silas," Drake said. "You have to let it go."

"Maybe you should let your little strumpet go instead. Get a real taste for how it feels to lose the person you love most in the world at the hands of someone else."

Fire erupted in Drake's belly, churning into an inferno of rage. "You touch a hair on her head and I swear on our father's grave that I will hunt you down like the dog you are.

When I'm done with you, you'll be begging for mercy."

"Ha! You don't even know where the hell I am now! How do you expect to find me to finish this plan of yours?"

Silas belted out a laugh that echoed through the boardroom. "I think the rumor about Luminaries is true. They do make Alphas batshit crazy."

"Fuck you," Drake spat.

"I'm gonna make you a deal, *brother*." Silas leaned toward the camera until his sneering face filled the screen. "You hand over control of our father's pack, declare in front of everyone that you are conceding to my rule, that I am the Alpha and rightful heir to the throne, and I'll let your precious Emelia live."

The floor beneath Drake's feet slipped away. His legs dangled over the edge of his chair, going numb from the toes up as the feeling of being swept away on a rogue wind dizzied him. Blood pounded against his temples and rushed through his ears.

He couldn't deal with the devil. He just couldn't. Once Silas ruled the pack, he'd have more power than he'd know what to do with. His blame and hatred wouldn't stop. Silas would focus the army of the pack on Drake no matter what he said or did. In order to protect Emelia, Drake needed to stay in control. He needed the protection of the pack and to keep their strength out of Silas's hands.

"I'll always love you, Silas," Drake said, fighting back a snarl. "And I wish it wasn't like this…but you've just sealed your fate."

He disconnected the call before Silas asked for everything.

"Raul, have the men go back over this tape. Look for any clues. Sounds, flinches, cues, *anything* that might give a clue as to where he's headed. Keep me posted on the flight information that comes from the ground."

"Will do." Raul nodded and wildly scribbled a note on the

pad of paper in front of him.

Shoving his arms into his coat, trying not to think about the family ties he'd just severed, Drake marched to the door. Damn it, he'd almost forgotten about the planning for Emelia's bar; he'd spread himself too thin this time. "And Raul, I need you to reschedule the business meetings from this afternoon to Monday. I have to take the rest of today to finalize the deal for Emelia's bar."

Raul met Drake at the door. "I thought you said you were leaving the lawsuit in her hands."

"I am," Drake said as rain battered the windows in a relentless onslaught. "I'm talking about the other bar. The one that'll make her forget all about the Knight Owl."

"I'm sorry if this is overstepping my grounds, sir, but I overheard one of her guards talking…"

Shit, here it comes.

"From my understanding of what I heard, you told Emelia that a female turned werewolf wouldn't be able to survive having an Alpha's child."

Drake exited the office and nodded to Trixie on the way down the hall. "I hate to focus on responding to your comment, when I should be focused on smacking the hell out of her guards for talking behind our backs, but yes. I informed Emelia of the predicament. I thought it was the right thing to do…for her to know what kind of a future she faced with me."

"Begging my pardon, sir," Raul said, pressing the elevator door button. "But who told you about that…predicament?"

The elevator doors opened and they swept inside.

"My father," Drake said, folding his arms over his chest. "I remember hearing rumors about females dying while I was in training in the Sierras."

"Forgive me for saying so, sir, but your father was wrong."

Drake's gaze shot to Raul. "What are you talking about?"

"My cousin Veronica was turned by her husband, the

Alpha of his pack in New Mexico. They have five beautiful, healthy children, and she'll be three hundred and two next month."

"Son of a bitch." He'd *lied*. "Why would he lie about something like that?"

Drake didn't need an answer. His father had always believed turned werewolves were weaker, and would never be as strong as pure-blooded, born wolves. He'd never wanted his sons to bond for love. He'd wanted them to bond for strength and the strong succession of the pack.

He had *brainwashed* them.

Emelia would be able to have his children. His heirs. They could build their future with or without children, but at least now they had the choice.

As the elevator doors hissed shut, Drake's heart skipped a beat.

Chapter Seventeen

By the time Emelia shut off the lights in the bar, it was just past 2:00 a.m. The night had been slow. Slower than she'd ever seen on a Friday night. Were the other businesses in the area being affected the same way? She'd counted one thousand dollars in the till. Much less than it should've been, even for the weekend before Thanksgiving.

Emelia flipped up her hood and made her way outside, following the three packmates who seemed to be stuck to her side like glue. Drake's black convertible Roadster was parked against the curb, its soft-top in place, its windshield wipers sloshing rain onto the sidewalk. Drake exited his car, circled the front, and met them under the awning.

"I've got things from here, gentlemen," Drake said, his dark, brooding eyes flickering from one packmate to another. "Thank you for your service tonight."

"No problem, sir," Logan said with a curt nod. He turned his attention to Emelia. "If there's anything else you need from me, Ms. Hudson, don't hesitate to let me know. I left my card on the bar."

Drake grabbed Logan by the scruff of his neck. "In case you didn't understand, I said beat it."

Logan nodded, and Drake released his hold.

"You didn't have to do that," Emelia said as her bodyguards strode to the public parking lot across the street. "He's just trying to be helpful."

"There's a fine line between helpful and...*helpful*." He wiggled his eyebrows up and down. "He knows what I'm talking about, and he knows I'm only half-serious."

Drake was officially jealous. Emelia's pride swelled.

"You know," she said, locking up, "it's a good thing he's being the first kind of helpful, the one before the eerie eyebrow dance."

Drake laughed as Emelia scanned the sidewalk, looking for signs of a stranger, a werewolf—*someone* who would jump out from between the buildings and attack her. The last time she'd come out of her bar at this hour, one of Silas's packmates had been there, ready to take her head off. Although Emelia didn't see anyone around, the creepy, hair-on-end feeling that someone was watching her remained as strong as ever.

"How'd it go tonight?"

"Good," she lied.

She turned around and caught her breath. She hadn't noticed Drake's attire. He was dressed in dark-washed jeans, a stone-gray sweater, and combat boots. He was drenched, his dark hair sticking to his forehead in wet strands. For the first time, Drake had opted out of his stuffy suit and tie, or his pressed-straight polo shirts and slacks. Emelia fought the smile tweaking the corners of her mouth. He didn't dress up for their date. At least not in the way she'd expected him to. This was better.

Somehow, from a few brief seconds at her side, Drake eased the tension in Emelia's shoulders and settled the anxiety swirling in her stomach. She felt safe with him. Like no one would be able to touch a hair on her head with him around.

"Have you been waiting out here long?" she asked, pocketing her keys.

"No, just got here. I had some business to take care of earlier that consumed my day." It was clear that he wanted to say more, but didn't.

"Want to talk about it?" she asked.

"Not really. Everything's being handled properly. I'm just looking forward to spending tonight with you to get my mind off things."

Palming the small of her back, Drake led Emelia to his car, opened the door and waited for her to settle into the leather seat. He really was a gentleman, wasn't he? Probably one of the only few left in the world. He slid into the driver's seat and brought the car roaring to life. She took Drake's hand as he gripped the stick shift. His skin was wet but warm, and her hand molded into his perfectly. Just the way she knew it would.

"So where are we going on this first date of ours?" she asked.

"You ask a lot of questions, you know that? I told you earlier, it's a surprise." The car lurched forward as he slammed it into gear and peeled out, leaving the worries of the night far behind them. "Hold on."

She gripped the "oh-shit" handle on the doorframe as Drake drove the BMW hard, handling it masterfully around curves, flooring it when they had room on the road, and stopping at lights without a single jar. Emelia couldn't help but throw her head back, laughing from her belly when Drake slowed for passing cops and then sped around the next corner without looking back. Once they hit the freeway and followed signs to Auburn, Drake really let loose, revving the engine to its max, speeding down the slick roadway like he owned it.

When they exited fifteen minutes later, Emelia was smiling so hard that her cheeks hurt.

"How is it possible that you're so uptight in the boardroom," Emelia said, as he gunned the car around a tight corner, "and so reckless on the road?"

"I've always loved cars. I should show you the muscle cars in my garage back home."

Muscle cars? So it wasn't about speed or recklessness at all. It was about power. The Drake Wilder Puzzle fit together before her eyes. Suddenly, it wasn't so surprising that he owned a ton of cars and drove like a bat out of hell. He owned a bunch of companies and ruled over a pack, too. It shocked Emelia how easily she was starting to be able to figure him out.

"At least now I know why you take the limo everywhere," Emelia teased.

"Why's that?"

"You're hell on wheels! Do you know how many tickets I'd have if I drove like this all the time?"

"Two," he said, giving her a knockout smile. "One for going sixty-five in a forty-five zone and the other for not wearing a seat belt."

She smacked him in the shoulder playfully. "Your background checks sure are thorough, aren't they?"

"Not thorough enough for my taste." His hand slid up her thigh, leaving a trail of goose bumps behind. Her legs parted on their own accord, willing his hand to continue its trek.

When they pulled into a drive-in a few turns later, Emelia swore she'd died and gone to heaven. She'd never been to a drive-in and had always wanted to go. The place looked like it had been awesome in its heyday, with overgrown lawn lining the edges of the parking pad, a swing set near the screen, and picnic tables beneath a spattering of leafless trees.

"Seriously?" she said, mouth dropping open in disbelief.

"There's a show playing now? This late at night?"

"For us, there is." Drake rounded the corner of a deteriorating snack shack and parked in a stall near the enormous blank screen. "One of my packmates had a vision for the lot and wanted to buy it. The numbers were right, so Wilder Financial invested in the property, and he was kind enough to let me rent it for the night."

"Wow." There were no other words. The lot was barren, leaving sound-posts sticking out of the ground like flower stems robbed of their petals. "I thought they did away with these things. Don't they have the sound from the movie play through the radio?"

"I don't think he's had a chance to renovate the place yet." Drake turned off the engine and smiled as the quiet patter of raindrops ceased to fall on the softly padded roof. "Perfect timing."

Drake peeled back the convertible top and let it drop behind them. He rolled down the windows, unhooked the speaker from its stand, and hung it on the door. They wouldn't get a reprieve from the rain for long, but maybe it would hold out long enough to watch the movie.

"Okay, now this is fucking cool." Emelia squirmed in her seat. Although clouds still cluttered the sky, the rain had stopped and the wind had died. "What's playing?"

"*Sabrina*." With a smile, he popped the trunk and exited the car. "I'm a Bogart fan and thought you might like it. Have you seen the original version?"

"I've seen the newer one with Harrison Ford," she said, thinking back to whether or not she liked it. If the movie was a downer, she could think of other things to do with Drake in an empty parking lot. "Is the original black and white?"

"Of course. It released in the fifties."

She suppressed a groan, but dropped her head back against the seat. Black-and-white movies put her to sleep.

"We can watch something else." Drake tossed two fuzzy blankets onto her lap and returned to the front seat. "I've got *Teen Wolf* on standby."

"Hardy-har."

As the screen came to life, rich in its shades of black, gray, and white, Emelia draped the blankets over their laps and snuggled against Drake's shoulder. Within minutes her disappointment eased. She was at a drive-in watching a movie beneath a cloudy sky with the man of her dreams. Who cared if they watched a black-and-white movie or the newest hit?

Excitement bubbled inside her. It wasn't the warmth of his body, the buzz of the coffee she'd had before leaving the bar, or watching a movie this way that had her heart beaming with light.

It was *him*.

Realization struck Emelia as Audrey Hepburn's voice flowed from the speaker and into the car. She could be in his mansion or her teeny-tiny apartment, his yacht or an inflatable raft, beneath a starry sky or balloons of rainclouds…as long as she was with Drake, she'd be happy.

Damn, if she wasn't in love with the business-suit-wearing, classic-movie-loving, richer-than-gravy werewolf.

Chapter Eighteen

"He should give it all up and go to her," Emelia said, choking back the emotion welling inside her. Her gaze was glued to the screen. The movie was almost over, and her heart was wrenching. "Why is Linus being so blind? Why won't he admit his feelings to himself? He loves her."

"Yes, he does," Drake said, "but he's been taught to follow his logic for so long that he's become deaf to the voice in his heart telling him that she's his match."

"Then he needs to wake his ass up." She swiped a tear rolling down her cheek. "He's going to lose her and she's perfect for him."

"She is perfect for him, but what good will it do Linus to declare his love if Sabrina insists on denying her own feelings?"

"What are you talking about? Look at them." She pointed to the larger-than-life screen. "Deep down Sabrina has to know she loves him."

Her words silenced Drake, and when she searched his face for the reason, it struck her. He wasn't talking about the movie at all. He was talking about them. About Emelia turning Drake down, and turning him away.

She looked at him then, her stomach in a giant knot, her heart overflowing with joy and sadness and…love. Their gazes locked. Emelia's heart overflowed with desire. Drake wasn't her boss, the owner of half of Seattle, and probably one of the wealthiest men on the planet. Well, he *was* those things, but he wasn't those things to her. He was just a guy with the plushest lips she'd ever seen. A guy who made her skin tingle and her heart skip beats. He was a guy who laughed at her crazy jokes, and made her feel like a princess…a princess who could rule her own kingdom if she wanted to.

She wanted him. *This* man. The one sitting beside her. And she wanted him no matter which package he came in. No matter if their future held children or not.

"Kiss me, Drake," she said.

He angled his body toward her, hesitating, gazing at her as if he knew, as if he felt the snapping in her middle. When Emelia opened her mouth to say more, Drake devoured her words, his lips on hers, his hands brushing feather-softly over her cheeks.

Everything slipped away but the sweet, succulent taste of Drake's mouth and the electricity behind his touch. Tremors worked through her, tingling her toes, buzzing through her legs, and gathering in her middle. Tangling his hands in her hair, Drake sighed into her and tilted Emelia's head to deepen the kiss.

She was on fire for him. Burning.

As if he read her mind, Drake palmed her breasts, kneading them in his hands. Her skin caught fire beneath her sweater. She arched back and severed their kiss, then slipped the sweater over her head, exposing a black lace bra that Drake wasted no time raking his fingers against.

"You're so beautiful." His words were fragments, pushed

out breathlessly. "Perfect."

Unable to hold back, Emelia dove into another kiss, slanting her mouth over his. As she slid to the edge of her seat and leaned into him, coiling her arms around his neck, Emelia realized it wouldn't be enough. Her hand found his chest, traipsed down a set of washboard abs, and stroked the bulge in his jeans. He groaned in approval, his hips rising off the seat as his tongue swirled along hers.

Still. Not. Enough.

Desperation rising, Emelia tugged Drake's sweater over his head and clawed her nails down the sculpted muscles of his chest. He hissed, forcing a quick breath of air through his teeth.

"Did I hurt you?" she asked, biting her lip as she gazed at the ridges on his stomach.

"Baby," he said, his dark eyes burning with wicked intention, "you can't hurt me."

"Is that so?" She leaned over the console and clawed into the hard, muscular groove at his waist, then rubbed her hands over his slick, tanned skin. He bit his own lip and let his head drop back onto the headrest. With her other hand, Emelia stroked his bulge harder, writhing as her own desire spiked, drenching her panties in warmth.

Creating friction over their clothes wasn't going to cut it. They were beyond that.

In a fevered rush, Emelia kicked off her shoes and unbuttoned her pants. She shuffled out of them, panties in tow, and flicked them onto the floorboard. Drake followed her lead, unzipping his pants and jerking them down along with his boxers. When Drake leaned back into the seat, his erection bobbed against his stomach, its thick head swelling over his belly button. She'd never wanted to take a man in her mouth this way—it had never been her thing—but now, she couldn't think of anything else.

She wanted to pleasure him like he'd pleasured her the last time they made love.

"Ever have sex in a car, Drake?" Emelia asked, wetting her lips.

He smiled slyly. "Not with you."

"Clever man." She bent over and took the hard length of him in her mouth, then pulled back and licked the tip. He trembled—it was a tiny, quivering movement, but she caught it. "You always know just what to say."

He sucked in a shocked breath as she worked her tongue around his head and massaged the base of him with her hand. He moaned. Thrust his hips gently in time with her strokes, and when his torso went rigid, Emelia knew she had him right where she wanted him. As if Emelia's body could sense Drake's rising pleasure, her chest tightened and her breath hitched. She was all sensation, crazed and drawn tight. She was ready to ride him, aching to let him fill her with his seed. She was ready to explode. One touch and she'd come apart.

Using the steering wheel and the back of Drake's seat for balance, Emelia moved from her seat to Drake's lap. Her knees barely fit on either side of him, but they fit enough. She situated herself over him, feeling their sexual chemistry spark across her skin.

"Did you bring protection this time?" She suckled his earlobe into her mouth.

He groaned and skated his hands up and down her back. Groping greedily at her hips, Drake said, "Diseases don't pass from werewolves to humans, though I'm clean anyway, and you have to be like me—I mean, you have to have shifted into a werewolf already—to be able to get pregnant."

"Really? I get to feel you skin-to-skin?" Slowly, she wriggled her core over his tip, and latched her arms around his neck. "You just made my day."

"Hell, woman, you just made my life," Drake said,

unsnapping her bra, slipping it off her shoulders and flinging it onto the passenger seat. "I want to be inside you so bad. Tell me I can make you come this way. Give me the words, baby."

Odd as it was, Emelia was beginning to like the whole "asking permission" thing before sex. Although she could never imagine an instance when she'd turn Drake down, it was empowering to know that he respected her enough to ask first.

"I'll give you any words you want. Take me hard. Right now. Is that what you want to hear?" She impaled herself over him, groaning in time with Drake as his head dropped back. A tumbling wave of ecstasy crashed over Emelia, dragging her to the edge of release. "Oh, Drake, yes!"

"I want more." Drake softly kissed her breasts, nipping and licking, leaving a scorching trail of wet heat behind. "Tell me you're mine."

She rolled her hips slowly, fighting the urge to pound against him and drive him deeper inside her. "I'm yours."

"That's it." As a gust of wind swept over the car, Emelia's hair flew wildly about her face. Catching the flying strands of blond, Drake yanked her head back and exposed her neck. He claimed her with his mouth, smudged kisses down her neck, sucked and bit at her shoulder. He thrust deep inside, plunging deeper than Emelia thought possible.

The wind whipped around them harder, and as rain began to sprinkle Emelia's face, the thrill of the night overtook her. She rode Drake hard, gasping, begging, grinding her hips over him mercilessly. The harder she pounded her hips over him, the tighter he gripped her. The sight of Drake sprinkled with sweat and rain, his dark hair plastered to his forehead, his muscles flexing and pulsing…it was too much.

She wanted to cry out at the sheer bliss of the moment. She wanted to scream. Claim Drake Wilder as her own. She wanted to growl and claw and bite, which was all kinds of crazy considering she'd never experienced such primal impulses before.

"I want to bond with you, Emelia," he bit out, swaying her hips in a torturous rhythm.

"You are bonding with me." She kissed him, slipping her tongue past his lips, desperate to taste more of his mouth.

"No," he said, in between gasps of air. "I want to complete the bond with you. I want you to be my Luminary."

She stilled, aware of every falling drop of rain, every twitch and pulse of his shaft in her core, every stuttering heartbeat.

"There's something else, too." Drake gripped her sides, holding her still over the top of him.

"Give it to me."

"I was wrong about not being able to have children. I was lied to." He gazed deep into her eyes, catching her heart. "We don't have to, if you don't want to, but at least we'll have the choice."

"You mean we could start a family someday?" She tasted the sweetness of the words. "Oh, Drake, yes. I wanted to be with you, for us to be together, with or without children. I'd planned to tell you tonight. But now…my heart is bursting. I couldn't ask for anything more."

The passion in his kiss increased until Emelia thought she'd melted into him, her skin heated up and scorched through.

"What will the bonding mean?" she asked, beginning to move her hips once more. "We'll be married?"

"Yes." A throaty moan escaped him. "It's a werewolf's equivalent of marriage, but if you want a traditional ceremony after this, we can arrange it. But not now."

"No." She bit her lip, sliding her wet breasts against his chest, craving the contact. "Not now."

Would she even want a marriage ceremony? She wasn't sure of much when his body was beneath hers this way. But she knew she wanted a future with Drake—a family, home, and children just like him. No wait, their children would be a meshing of the both of them. Wild meshed with reserve. Smart with savvy. It'd be perfect.

"I'll love you forever," Drake said, and raised her hand to meet his. "Palm to palm, heart to heart, from this day forward, we shall never part."

"That was beautiful." She kissed him. "I love you, too."

"Say it," he whispered.

"Palm to palm, heart to heart..." She shuddered. "From this day forward, we shall never part."

As the words left her lips, Drake kissed her with all the passion he had inside. Emelia could feel his offering, though she couldn't explain how. She matched it, pinching her eyes shut, giving every last ounce of her heart and soul to him. His tongue swept into her mouth as his shaft swelled inside her. In that instant, Emelia's soul shattered into a thousand brilliant pieces, sparkling through her body like shooting stars in the night sky. Drake cried out, clutching on to Emelia's back, plunging his tongue past her lips, thrusting deep, so deep inside.

They had become one. Emelia knew it with every heavy thump of her heart.

They were bonded.

Emelia, Drake said, his voice husky.

"Yes."

Look at me.

She opened her eyes, held the gaze of her life-mate, and smiled. "Yes?"

I promise to take care of you like the queen you are, he said, though his lips didn't move.

Her eyebrows pinched. "How—"

"Call it another benefit to becoming a werewolf."

"You can hear my thoughts?" She was in trouble now.

"Only when you project them." He kissed her the way she'd always dreamed of being kissed. Like he'd die without her. Like he needed her more than the breath passing his lips. "The inner workings of your brain will remain yours."

"Thank God."

She'd never felt more full of life, and love, than she did at this moment. As Drake began to knead her rear once more, Emelia fell back into a slow, seductive rhythm. It didn't take long before kisses turned heated, playful nips turned to bites, and Emelia was slammed back against the steering wheel so Drake could ravish her breasts.

He drove his hand between their bodies, and when he reached her silken heat, he teased her, lightly circling his fingers where she ached and tingled and wanted more pressure. He played her as though her body was an instrument...one he was skilled at strumming. Her muscles seized. Her body trembled. He increased the swirling tempo of his fingers as her hips rolled, leading her toward the blissful release she so desperately craved. The pressure in Emelia's core gathered into a white-hot ball of ecstasy, building, cresting, and then— she exploded, rising and falling in brilliant white light. Her vision blurred, her toes curled, and her hamstrings cramped.

"Drake..." His name rushed out of her, and before she knew it, she was thrown into another orgasm that was more powerful than the first. The pleasure was so great, she cried out over and over again, Drake's name ripping from her throat uncontrollably.

"Emelia," Drake breathed. "You're mine. Forever."

"Yes."

As Emelia's center gave a final, fading pulse, Drake clenched, going rock-hard from jaw to cock. He gripped Emelia's shoulders as his hips rose in a final resounding push. When his orgasm hit, he stared deep into Emelia's eyes and surged into her over and over again, filling her with warmth.

Finally, they stilled. Rain continued to fall, dusting a cool mist over their weak, spent bodies. Emelia let her arms fall to her sides and her chest rested against him…her *husband*. Is that what Drake was considered now? She'd have to ask him if the same titles applied in his pack.

Drake wrapped his arms around her tightly and exhaled. The sound of soft music wafted from the speaker next to Emelia's ear. The movie had ended and the credits were rolling.

"You were right," she said, struggling to catch her breath. "That was a great movie."

He stroked her hair. "Best I've ever seen."

"By far."

Using two fingers, Drake tilted Emelia's chin to him. His eyes shone with more love and awe than Emelia deserved. How could she have been so stupid as to deny her feelings before? She loved this man through and through.

"Want to watch it again?" He winked, causing her heart to stutter.

"This time," she said, "let's watch it at your place."

Chapter Nineteen

"Do you pull all-nighters often?" Emelia asked as they pulled into a Starbucks in Beacon Hill, a quaint area in southern Seattle.

"Not usually." He zipped through the drive-through, stopping when they reached the order sign. "But tonight's a special occasion. There's something I want to show you."

Doing a little dance inside, Emelia checked the time on the dash. 5:00 a.m. She may have been used to staying up late, but even this was pushing it. Surprisingly, she wasn't tired. Not with Drake sitting beside her, massaging her thigh, gazing at her like he wanted to do naughty things with her in the backseat…if only Roadsters had backseats, damn it.

As Drake rolled down the driver's-side window, Emelia leaned across the center console and peered at the glowing sign. Drake's body radiated heat, his chest resting against hers, his breath coating her ear in a deliciously warm wave.

"Welcome," a male's voice greeted, much too chipper for the early hour. "What can I get you?"

"A grande—" Emelia yelped as Drake's palm patted the

round of her backside and his teeth grazed her ear. "Stop that." Emelia glared into Drake's mischievous eyes. Her chest warmed and her blood quickened its rush through her veins. "I'm sorry," she said into the speaker, leaning further over the car's stick shift. "I'd like a grande quadruple—"

"I'd like to give you a quadruple shot," Drake whispered, then spanked her with a loud *smack!*

Emelia screamed as she lurched forward, then fell back into her seat. "Do you want me to order or not?" she said, unable to fight the laughter bubbling within her.

Drake nodded, and tucked his hands beneath his legs. "From now on, I'll be on my best behavior."

Eyeing him skeptically, Emelia leaned forward once more. "Sorry about that," she yelled. "I'd like a grande quadruple zebra mocha, and a—" Stopping, Emelia met Drake's eyes. They'd turned from playful to lustful in a heartbeat. "What do you want?"

"You know what I want." The words were a cat's purr, deep and rumbling off his tongue.

Hell yes, she knew what he wanted. And she wanted the same thing.

Using one of the hands that were supposed to be on lockdown, Drake massaged Emelia's back, then swept around her waist and dipped between her legs. Emelia's breath whooshed out of her lungs and her mouth dried. As Drake stroked the juncture between her thighs, Emelia realized she really didn't need air to refill her lungs. Air was seriously overrated. As long as Drake kept doing—oh God, *that*—she'd be fine.

"I'd also like a grande black coffee." Emelia's eyes fluttered closed as Drake's fingers swirled teasingly over the seam in her jeans. She spread her legs and arched her back, earning a groan of approval from Drake's lips. She went damp from his touch, and began to quiver with need.

"You should change your drink to a venti," Drake said, a little too loud. "Once you hear all the kinky things I'm going to do to you, you'll want to be up all damn day."

"Uh, thanks for the offer, sir," the man from the speaker blurted, "but I don't get off work until two this afternoon."

Drake and Emelia erupted with laughter, and didn't stop until they'd paid for their drinks, handsomely tipped the eager barista, and put Starbucks in the rearview.

...

"I left my coffee in the car," Emelia said. "Don't you trust that I can be blindfolded, walk, and drink coffee at the same time?"

She tripped over a sidewalk curb and stumbled, latching on to Drake's arm before her nose met the concrete.

"Not hardly." Drake hauled her against him. "I'll get your coffee for you in a second. Just hold on to me for now. You're going to love what I'm about to show you, I promise. After this we'll go back to my place. I'll make you breakfast in bed and we can roll around in the sheets all day."

Sounded like perfection if she'd ever heard it.

Drake had blindfolded Emelia with the tie he'd pulled out of the glove compartment. The instant he draped it over her eyes, she breathed in. It smelled like him—spicy and rich. She had no clue exactly where they were, or what was going on, but as long as she was with Drake, she really didn't care.

"Another step up," he said, helping her over a stoop. "And another."

"Drake, what's going on?" Her voice squeaked a bit, and she hated it.

Keys jingled. A door swept open, drenching them in the sweet scent of espresso and...was that the spicy, pungent smell of seasoned fish? Drake escorted Emelia over a threshold and into some sort of large space that echoed the stomping of his boots as they walked deeper inside. The place was warm and took away the chill from Emelia's bones immediately. And from the peeking space between Drake's tie and her nose, Emelia could tell the floor was hardwood. Glossy and probably slippery.

"Okay, Emie," Drake said, releasing her arm. "I know you're going to freak out when you see what's in front of you, but you have to promise to hear me out."

"Can I at least see what's in front of me while I'm listening?" She reached out her hands as she took another step forward and bumped into a clunky piece of furniture.

"All right." He was proud, his voice stern and commanding. "Go ahead."

Uncertain as hell, Emelia slipped the tie over her head... and stared at a bar full of mirrors and pink decor, twinkling lights, bulky tables, and gold-rimmed barstools. In the back of the bar, an espresso station had been set up, and next to that, a spit-shield guarding what looked like a sushi stand.

Smiling, Drake spread his arms to his sides like a grandmaster emcee. "What do you think?"

"Umm," she said, biting her thumbnail. "What do I think about what?"

"Your new bar."

Oh, hells to the no.

"What do you mean by new—new as in, you bought this place for *me*?" Confusion and anger surged through Emelia's veins, but she clamped down the emotions, certain she'd missed something.

Drake nodded and charged around the long, sweeping bar, to where the bartender would stand serving drinks. The top tier racks were full, overflowing onto the ones below. "It's called Cosmo's. It's in a great area and the prior owner ran the place phenomenally. The neighboring businesses are rising and the climate is well-to-do, but not fussy. Right now the place is set up to serve wine, liquor, coffee, sushi, and what one might consider 'bar food,' though you could really change the menu however you wanted it once you got settled. So… what do you think? It's perfect, right?"

"What the hell, Drake?" Emelia's chest seized. This wasn't what she wanted. "We've been bonded for what, an hour? You're buying me property already? What were you thinking?"

She spun around, absorbing every glowingly irritating detail in the room. Bright-pink illuminated martini glasses perched over the mirror behind the bar, matching the decals on the walls on the front and sides of the room. The espresso machine gurgled, matching the souring in her middle.

"I purchased it last week and got a hell of a deal," he said proudly. He folded his arms and leaned over the bar. "Emelia, I saw the profits and losses for the Knight Owl. People from Wilder Financial have researched other businesses on the street. I know you've put your heart and soul into that place, but I just don't see it working."

She chuckled exasperatedly, though what she really wanted to do was rip the martini glass off the wall and slam it against Drake's head so he'd listen to what she'd been saying for the past few weeks. "So you thought you'd just sell my bar before it goes under completely, and have me manage this one instead?"

"It'd be a smart business move to sell it, Emie," he said, coming around the bar to stand beside her. He draped his arm over her shoulder and gazed at the exposed rafters as if it was some kind of majestic painting. "Look at this place—the mirrors, the various food and drink bars, the options for customers. It's exactly what people want."

"It's exactly what yuppies want!" she yelled, coming apart inside. "This place has zero personality."

"That's not true. Look, there's a poster of Marilyn Monroe over there."

"Yeah, I see her." Emelia chomped on her bottom lip. "I also see the velvet zebra-stripe frame she's stuck in. Come on, Drake, seriously? If this isn't a joke, I'm going to kill you where you stand."

Removing his arm from around her shoulder, Drake took a step back. "Listen, I know you're holding on to the Knight Owl because you put so much time and money into the place and it's hard to let go of a sour investment, but you've got to look at this from a purely business standpoint. This move makes sense."

"It makes sense for who, Drake?" Brazen annoyance licked through her insides, heating her skin until she thought she'd combust. "For you?"

He slapped his hands against his sides. "I thought you'd be happy."

"I don't want to run just any ole bar in Seattle, Drake. I want *my* bar."

"This is your bar now too, except this one is going to succeed."

Emelia flinched. That one stung. "If I *did* want another bar, which I don't, I'd want one with color and depth and warmth. One that stands out from the crowd, built in a historic building with newspaper clippings on the wall. I'd want a bar that's different, with a unique feel. This one feels cold, like it has no heart at all."

His expression hardened. "Then take it over and add your usual Emelia flair to it. Make it your own. At least the business is already thriving so you won't have to struggle the way you are now. You would have the money to step in and change it to make it fit whatever you want."

"You don't get it." She couldn't breathe in this place. Her chest was tight, her throat constricting. She backed away, closer to the exit and farther from Drake. "I want my bar because I clawed and fought my way to get it. I want it because I built it on my own, from the ground up. Because of all I've done for the place, I have a greater sense of pride when I see it do well, or when I see a good review of it online. No one can take that joy away from me."

"Your buddy Needles took it away easy enough."

"You ass." She stormed him, standing on tiptoe to stare into his smoldering brown eyes. "How dare you throw that in my face."

"It's the truth."

"You know, maybe you're right. Maybe I'm too stupid to fit into your business-minded world." She didn't feel stupid, she felt foolish. She'd been right before. They didn't fit together. They were too different.

He reached out for her, but dropped his hand. "Emelia, I didn't say you were stupid, it's just that we're arguing about apples and oranges. Joy doesn't always have to come from fighting your way through something. If you take a chance on a business and it does well, you celebrate and enjoy that victory. If something doesn't do well, you cut your losses and move on."

Frustration soured Emelia's stomach. "You talk about this stuff like it's so distant from you. Like you don't really care what you own as long as it turns a profit."

"I don't understand why you insist on holding on to something that's crumbling in your hands."

That was it. Emelia couldn't stand there while he kept hopping over a line that he shouldn't have crossed to begin with. Not tonight. "The Knight Owl might not crumble if I give it all I have," she said.

"After what just happened at the drive-in, I thought we'd do everything together. Guess I was wrong." Drake went rigid, leaning against one of the exposed wooden support posts standing oddly in the center of the room. "Damn it, Emelia, this place was an investment in our future together. I didn't just buy this bar for you, I bought it for both of us."

"That's just it," she seethed. "You said it yourself. Right there. *I* bought the bar. *For* you. I don't need you to do anything for me."

"So I can't buy my wife anything or she won't be able to enjoy it?" His voice boomed so loud it rattled the mirror against the wall behind her. "Do you know how ridiculous that sounds?"

"You know what's ridiculous, Drake?" As deep-rooted anger flared and burned inside her, Emelia let her frustration fly. "The fact that you now have control over your father's pack because we bonded tonight and—"

"We're going there again, are we?"

She glowered, fuming, ears burning.

His eyes rolled. "Continue."

"Like I was saying," she bit out. "I've probably made you one of the most powerful men on the planet, yet you can't seem to let me have the *one thing* I've worked so hard for."

"That's what you want, isn't it? This whole time, all you've wanted was for me to just hand over your bar, and give it to you on a damned silver platter."

"No!" *Why didn't he understand?* "I want you to acknowledge the fact that you're dodging things. Once again, the expert dodger is ignoring the big-ass elephant in the room."

"I'm so tired of having to interpret what you say all the time. Would you just spit it out and say what you mean? In English?"

Emelia shook her head, hands clenching into fists. "You think I'm ridiculous, that I'm just some blond bimbo who's better off as your secretary than a business owner. You think my decisions don't make sense. How about this, I'm going to lay it all out on the line for you."

"I'm holding my breath." Drake waved his hands in front of him in a give-it-to-me motion. "Come on, Emelia, out with it."

"You expect to have everything—the woman, the Luminary, the flourishing businesses, the yachts and mansions across the world—yet you sacrifice *nothing*. Not one fucking thing! But you expect *me* to sacrifice the one thing I've worked my ass off for, because you think it makes better sense to invest elsewhere. Well fuck you, Drake Wilder. Fuck you and the limo you rode in on."

"Real nice, Emelia." His jaw clenched wildly. "Why don't you stop before you say something you don't mean."

"Here's something I mean with all my heart." Her ears drummed with hot rushes of blood. "I'm going to give you a business tip…I don't do what I'm supposed to do. Ever. I don't think the way I should and I live my life swinging by my heartstrings. I'm probably the worst investment in a life partner that a guy like you could make."

"Emelia—" He came toward her, but she threw up her arms, and backed away.

"I won't let you ignore the fact that we don't fit together," she said. "I think this was a mistake."

His jaw clamped shut and his nostrils flared.

Cringing, Emelia averted her eyes. Why'd she just say that? She didn't mean it, not really. Damn it, now she couldn't look at him. "I gotta get out of here," she said, and stormed out the door.

• • •

What the hell just happened?

Drake stood motionless, his entire body pulsing with heated waves of anger. Emelia left. She just *left*. How could she walk out on him over a bar? A bar that was destined to fail, no less?

He charged into the street, but it was too late. Emelia was gone. *How'd she disappear so fast?* Retreating back into Cosmo's, Drake fumed, paced, walked from one side of the bar to the other as if it would do him good to stretch his legs.

Eyeing a bottle of scotch on the top tier, Drake scrubbed his hands through his hair, pulled down the bottle, and poured a stiff drink.

Damn it, he could still smell Emelia on his skin. He could still taste her, and feel her love filling him. Since they'd bonded, he could feel her like no other. It was like she was a part of him, no less important than an arm, a leg, or a chamber of his heart.

He loved her. She loved him. They were bonded for life. Then what the devil was the problem? How was offering Emelia a successful business wrong?

He shot the drink back, feeling worse than before. The scotch warmed his throat and buzzed down to his stomach, but the rage rattling his bones remained. He wanted to let the fire inside him erupt, chase Emelia down, clutch her by the shoulders and shake her until she understood.

"Like that would work, jackass!" He squeezed the glass and slammed it down so hard that it shattered. "She's not going to listen to reason."

He went palms-down over the bar and lowered his head. His jaw ached from clenching and his body shook from the force of his rage.

Emelia didn't get it. Drake had survived as long as he had because he was smart. Because he made wise decisions. Because he knew when to quit a business or invest in one. He rubbed his temples, pinching his thumb and forefinger together when piercing pain shot through his head like a flaming arrow.

Emelia hadn't asked for much, but what she did ask for was insane. It went against every bone in Drake's body. It went against three hundred years of training and education. Keeping the Knight Owl and investing more money and time into it was a waste. It was absurd.

For the first time in Drake's life, he didn't know how to fix the damn problem.

Women, he scoffed, pulling back his shoulders. Can't live with them, can't ship them off to a deserted island.

As he walked out the door to Cosmo's, he didn't look to see which direction Emelia might've gone. He got in his car and put the radio on full blast.

He couldn't do it. He *wouldn't* do it.

He would not invest in a business venture that would never go anywhere. He would not base his decisions on what he wanted to do over what he should do. He couldn't only think of himself and what he wanted. Now that he'd become a true Alpha, he'd lost that luxury.

With a sigh and the burden of his pack on his shoulders, Drake shoved the Roadster into gear and turned toward home.

Chapter Twenty

Emelia squirmed against the hand covering her mouth. The moment she'd stepped out of Cosmo's someone had grabbed her, dragging her into the alley next to the building. Her feet kicked and skidded as she fought against the man's abnormally strong hold.

This wasn't just any attacker—not that psychos had a telltale way they covered mouths and dragged bodies behind Dumpsters.

No, this guy smelled like wet hair and nasty dog slobber. *Wolf*, she corrected. Whoever it was had shifted recently.

"You're going to be silent," Silas said from behind her. "Or you're going to be dead, got me?"

She nodded, trying to control her breathing. She needed to keep her head clear, which meant she couldn't panic. Could. Not. Panic.

As Silas stuck the barrel of a weapon into Emelia's back, she froze. She didn't know a lick about guns, but common sense told her that the barrel of a gun should've been round. Whatever Silas had against her back was square.

Taser.

As the realization struck, Silas fired. Hard volts of electricity shot into Emelia's body. She fell to the concrete, paralyzed.

...

Drake hadn't talked to Emelia in three days. He'd explode if things kept going like this. He could feel Emelia, and sense her frustration and fear, but he couldn't be with her. She wouldn't answer his calls and she hadn't shown up for work Monday or Tuesday. As his Luminary, she was protected under pack law, but if she wouldn't answer the damn phone, how was he supposed to know where to send the security team? He'd sent them to her apartment after the fight at Cosmo's, but they'd reported back that she wasn't home.

His brother wouldn't be stupid enough to attack Emelia now. Not after he and Emelia had bonded. Silas might've been desperate enough to attack Emelia before, when she was alone and didn't have the protection of their pack, but now...he wouldn't do the one thing that would make him pack enemy numero uno.

The deal was done. Drake had become Alpha.

There was nothing Silas could do other than retreat and accept his fate.

Emelia was fine. In all likelihood she was irritated and pissed off, but safe.

The moon would be full tonight. Emelia would shift into a werewolf for the first time and would have to be taught how to handle her anger, how to channel it into the hunt, and how to shift back without experiencing any pain.

He'd sent Emelia an e-mail telling her about his cabin in neighboring Wenatchee Forest. His pack was ready to take her in with open arms. In fact, there was a caravan meeting at the ferry terminal this afternoon headed for the wilderness. They'd travel together, shift together, then return together when the full moon waned. They'd take good care of her… not like he could, but still.

Drake mulled over the thought of crashing the trip, but what good would that do? Emelia had made her decision clear.

They didn't fit. Her words still pierced him, days later.

The hollow ache in Drake's middle wouldn't ease, no matter how many Johnnie Walkers he downed. Two hard knocks on his office door startled him, but he didn't move from his chair.

"Come in," he said.

Trixie strode through the door and set a glossy coffee mug on Drake's desk. "Ms. Hudson didn't show up for work today either, Mr. Wilder. Would you like me to pull another temp into her position?"

Drake sipped his coffee. It tasted strange. Too bold. "I think that'd be best. No temp this time, though. Pull someone from another department."

"Will do." Trixie nodded, then nervously twirled a strand of russet-brown hair around her finger. "Sir, there's something I've been meaning to talk to you about."

"Shoot," Drake said, not really hearing her.

"We're missing some acquisitions reports from May of this year. I've searched for weeks and can't come up with anything. I had them on my desk when I began to train Ms. Hudson, but when I went looking for them a few days later, they were missing."

The reports weren't the only thing missing.

"Sir, they seem to have disappeared," she continued. "Don't you think that's strange?"

"Strange," he agreed, then took another drink of the coffee that still didn't taste right. "Trixie, would you throw this out and bring me my usual?"

He pushed the cup across his desk and continued to stare out the window, completely lost in thoughts of Emelia and the Knight Owl.

"That *is* your usual, sir," Trixie said. "There are only two pots of coffee that brew each day: regular and decaf. I didn't grab the wrong one. Maybe you've gotten used to how Emelia's been making it for you."

By the time Drake registered Trixie's words, she'd already made her way back into the hall. The door clicked shut quietly, leaving Drake alone with his thoughts.

Trixie was right.

Drake had gotten used to the way Emelia made his coffee, but it went deeper than that. He'd gotten used to the way she molded against him when he held her, the way she smiled playfully, lifting the weight off his shoulders. He'd gotten used to the way she brought laughter into his life. She didn't live on the straight and narrow, and she didn't make sense all the time. But he'd been out of balance before he met her. He'd been living a dull, boring life—one that was not really worth living to begin with.

Damn it.

He'd been an ass to buy her a new place. He'd been bullheaded, trying to force her into a certain conventional mold. It wasn't that Emelia didn't fit him, Drake realized. She simply didn't fit the mold he'd tried to place her in.

He loved her just the way she was.

Something heavy shifted in Drake's chest, feeling like a thunderous boom from a firework in an empty night sky. Emelia was his match in every way, and he hated that he made her doubt it.

He knew what he had to do.

Snatching a pen and paper from the top drawer of his desk, Drake scribbled a note that he should've written weeks ago, when he first learned that Emelia worked for him. He ripped the paper from its bed, folded it, and shoved it into his pocket. He made a quick call to Raul, who was out and about on business, then darted to the underground parking and slipped into his Roadster. His car seemed to drive itself to the Knight Owl, as if it too wanted to return to Emelia.

Once he pulled in front of the Knight Owl, Drake knew something wasn't right.

It was 9:00 a.m., and the bar should've been closed. Drake had only come here on a hunch; if Emelia wasn't home, maybe she'd been staying in her office. Emelia's car was parked out front, and an OPEN sign faced the front window. Every nerve in Drake's body sizzled at the sight. He growled, chewing on the feeling that the sign was for him.

Emelia wasn't alone in there.

Raging from muscle to bone, Drake charged around the car and burst through the door. A deafening howl ruptured from his chest when he caught Emelia's scared gaze. She'd been gagged and bound to a chair that sat on the stage in the corner. Her blue eyes screamed fear, clutching Drake's heart in an icy grip.

"Emelia!" he bolted into the room.

Movement to his right.

He crouched, knee to hardwood, as a burly gray wolf leaped through the air, aiming to take off Drake's head. Drake hit the wolf in the breastbone with his shoulder, and as it continued its arc over Drake's head, he stood quickly, tossing the snarling wolf onto the floor in a heap of writhing fur.

Another wolf charged at Drake from behind him. Drake waited, waited, waited for the perfect moment, then spun hard and fast, clocking the wolf in the snout with the lethally sharp ridge of his elbow.

This was too easy. He didn't even need to shift to knock

them down and out. But where was Silas? He had to have a hand in this.

"Hello, brother," Silas said as he emerged from around the wall separating the bar from the lounge. "Took you long enough to get here."

"Let her go, Silas." Drake fumed, barely able to control his breathing. "I'm only going to ask you once, and I suggest you listen while you can. The second time I speak, your head will be rolling on the floor."

"Temper, temper." Silas slowly approached the stage, his hands crossed behind him. "I'd hoped we could talk about this like gentlemen."

Metallic gray Duct tape had been smashed over Emelia's mouth and her hands had been tied behind her back, her ankles tied in front of her. If Silas touched another hair on her precious head it'd be the last thing he did…

"Are you all right?" Drake asked, focusing hard on the fear in Emelia's eyes.

Nodding quickly, Emelia took a few deep breaths through her nose, then shifted her gaze to whatever Silas was hiding behind his back. Drake wished Emelia had perfected the art of silent pack-speak, but nevertheless, he understood. Whatever weapon Silas held, it was worth warning him about.

"Fine," Drake said to Silas. "Let's talk. Call off your pups."

The two wolves that had attacked Drake snarled and spit, circling him like he was fresh meat at a feeding frenzy. As Silas spoke in his mind, the wolves backed away, but didn't go far. They stood against the edges of the room like well-taught soldiers, snorting puffs of air into the room.

"Hope you know that what you're doing is an act of war. Emelia and I completed the bonding ceremony. She is my Luminary through and through." Drake swallowed down the fear that he could lose her, so quickly after he'd found her. "Once my pack gets word of what you've done, it'll be open season on you and anyone you're associated with."

"Maybe your pack doesn't have to get word." Silas stood beside Emelia, stroking his hand down the back of her hair. She recoiled against his touch, cringing as he patted her head. "You see, Drake, I am not a monster—contrary to what you might think. I simply know that our father wouldn't have wanted a turned wolf to rule. I'm continuing his legacy."

"Those are the words of a madman," Drake said, stepping around a table to get closer. It would take him half a second to shift and leap to the stage. Would it be quick enough? "Our father lived in another time. Since fate brought Emelia to my side, maybe it's time we change the way we think. Maybe we should shift our pack mentalities a bit. Let her go."

"Not until I get what I want."

Silas tugged Emelia's head back. She yelped. Drake stalked closer. A single table separated them now.

"I told you my terms when we spoke earlier. They haven't changed. I want all of our father's estate," Silas said. "I want the land and property, the holdings, the bonds, the packmates who've been employed under his businesses, everything."

"You have everything. It's already passed to you."

Since Drake had become Alpha, Silas had inherited their father's estate. Drake had been left with the corporation he'd built...the Wilder Financial offices in Seattle and San Francisco. While he'd established the businesses well, they were nothing compared to the ones in their father's estate. They were nickels in a billion-dollar pot. There was no way Wilder Financial could support Drake's cost of living. He'd have to seriously downsize, nearly giving up everything. No jets. No multiple mansions. No extra staff. Bye-bye *Tara*, his grand yacht.

As Drake gazed into Emelia's eyes, his gut clenched. He'd give up anything to be with her, his life included. He'd sacrifice every last penny he earned to see her smile another day.

Emelia had been right earlier, but only partially. He expected everything and compromised nothing. *Except* when it came to her.

"I'm not going to fight you on a dollar of our father's money," Drake said. "It's yours."

Emelia made a squealing sound and squirmed against the ropes. Waves of frustration and anger flowed from Emelia's body, sparking against Drake's heightened senses. But mixed with those upsetting emotions came the unmistakable scent of adoration.

"I said everything, Drake." Silas sucked a breath of air through his teeth. "That means I get control over the pack, too."

"That's not happening."

"Then I'll kill your woman."

Rumbling came from deep within Drake's chest. "This is between us, Silas. It's always been between us. Why don't you do the honorable thing for once and leave my woman out of this." Drake growled, his body seizing into one giant knot.

"But she's the reason I'm in this position to begin with. If she's dead, you don't have a Luminary and you don't have heirs. When you're dead and gone, the pack will obey me."

"You're more insane than I suspected." Drake stalked closer. "I'm going to enjoy beating the sense back into you."

Silas crouched, his hands clenching into fists at his sides, his onyx eyes blazing like wicked fire. His eyes twitched and the wolves against the walls flexed, inching closer.

It didn't take a calculating mind to know that three wolves fighting against one were terrible odds.

Chapter Twenty-One

Everything stood still.

Drake scanned the furry faces of the wolf to his right, his left, anticipating their first strike. But when his gaze landed on Silas, and he read lethal intent in his brother's eyes, Drake growled, surging into attack mode. Silas drew his weapon quickly, shooting two electrically charged rods at Drake's chest. Drake ducked and spun out of the way as the electric strings buzzed through the air and scraped against the floor where he'd stood.

The wolves attacked, charging full speed to Drake's position. Emelia screamed, a strangled cry muffled by the tape. Silas yanked off the expended Taser cartridge and retrieved the second cartridge on the butt of the gun. Reloaded.

Wolf form or not, if Silas struck Drake with the Taser, he'd drop like a stone. Drake could dodge bullets in wolf form, which was probably why Silas chose a Taser rather than a Glock to try to bring Drake down. Hell, Drake could still rip someone's throat out with a bullet lodged in his flesh. But by the time Drake stopped twitching from the volts surging through his system, he'd be dead.

Drake saw each and every movement, each step clearer than the last.

As Silas took aim and the wolves closed in, Drake let the fury building inside him coil like a serpent in the pit of his stomach. When the pressure increased, tightening something in his chest into a hard knot, he roared. Muscles exploded over his back, arching his spine higher and higher into the air. His chest ballooned. His teeth sharpened to deadly canine points. He dropped to all fours as fur burst from his skin, blanketing his body in dark, coarse strands of wolf hair. He shook. Quivered with pent-up aggression.

Emelia jerked the chair toward the edge of the stage, struggling to get free from the ties around her hands and legs. It wouldn't be long now.

The wolf attacking from Drake's right commanded his attention. It must've sensed Drake's rage and unparalleled strength. It hesitated. A fraction of a second. Long enough for Drake to spring into action. He turned, took a single leap, and bared his fangs, chomping into the wolf's neck. With a whimper, the wolf dangled in Drake's teeth, its front legs going limp.

Silas shot off another Taser shot, but Drake's senses were on full alert. He could hear the rods whizzing through the air and bounded aside. Another miss.

He was running out of time.

Taking the kill shot while he had it, Drake snapped his jaws together, severing the wolf's carotid artery.

Sensing the death of its packmate, the second wolf roared and rushed behind Drake, hungry for vengeance. Drake spun, dropping the first wolf from his jaws, but didn't move quickly enough. The roaring wolf bit into Drake's side. Drake howled, arching, squirming to get the wolf's razor-sharp teeth out of his fur. With a violent shake, the wolf's canines dislodged from

Drake's flesh.

Adrenaline sparking through his veins, Drake crouched and spun, trying to get a lead on the wolf's weakness. The wolf matched Drake step for step, pounce for pounce.

Out of the corner of his eye, Drake saw Silas shift. He bulked up, rippling with layers of thick, corded muscle.

Damn it, it was now or never.

Drake reared up on his hind legs, slicing his paw across the wolf's muzzle. The wolf howled, blood trickling down its snout. Drake swiped his paw again, this time catching the wolf in the eye. Temporarily blinded, the wolf snapped for Drake and missed, leaving his neck vulnerable to attack. Drake took full advantage, bit through fur and flesh, and dropped the lifeless wolf to the hardwood.

As Drake spun around and met Silas's coal-black wolf eyes, he snarled, pulling back his lips to reveal his fangs. They hummed, tingling his gums. His back hunched. Silas snarled back, his snout dripping with saliva, his mangy black hair rising on end.

This was it. The moment Drake had dreaded since their father died. Deep down he had known it would come to this. Silas was greedy and spoiled sour to the core. Silas had simply been biding his time, waiting for this moment when he could challenge Drake for everything without the members of his pack viewing the action as disgraceful.

As Silas stalked around the table separating them, Drake backed away slowly, drawing him farther away from Emelia and closer to the center of the bar. Taking the upper hand, Drake lunged, propelling his body into Silas's. They hit with the force of giants, colliding into tables behind them and skidding over the floor. They tumbled and rolled, a mess of fur and teeth, biting and clawing their way to top position.

Silas had gotten stronger since Drake fought him last. He was quicker, too. More prepared for Drake's moves. He'd been practicing. Readying himself for this fight.

But Drake had some moves up his sleeve, too.

As they slammed into the wall, Drake managed to pin Silas beneath him with his back legs. Drake kicked and clawed with his forelegs, tearing through Silas's abdomen, and came away with gobs of bloody fur in his paws. Early pangs of victory hit Drake's system, but he didn't celebrate. Not yet. Drake's strikes were brutal. Lethal. But the angrier Drake seemed to get, the more Silas seemed to enjoy the fight. He batted away the heavy-pounding strikes of Drake's paws. Snapped at Drake's legs. Snorted when Drake missed a mark and rebounded with potentially fatal bites from his own snarling jaws.

It was all or nothing.

Drake went for the kill. With hundreds of years of repressed anger bubbling up inside him, Drake towered over Silas and dropped his muzzle like a hammer onto his neck. But Silas anticipated Drake's move. Before Drake could sink his fangs into Silas's flesh, Silas squirmed beneath him, knocking Drake off-kilter.

With a guttural groan, Silas snapped a meaty chunk out of Drake's neck.

Warm rushes of blood leached the strength from Drake's muscles.

Out of instinct alone, Drake darted away from Silas to assess his injuries. His breathing was ragged, his heavy heartbeats pounding against his rib cage like war drums. Blood oozed down Drake's neck, dripped down his chest, and flooded onto to the floor. If he didn't change back into human form soon, so his injuries could heal during the shift, he was liable to bleed out.

Emelia moaned breathlessly, dragging Drake's attention to the stage. Her icy blue eyes gripped him, reached through space between them, and struck him like a bolt of lightning.

He had to win this fight. For Emelia. For both of them.

Silas attacked, charging with newfound strength. Drake bounded aside, but he'd lost too much blood. His reactions were slowed, his instincts muddled. Silas slammed into him, knocking Drake to the ground. Drake refused to be on his back, so he scrambled. Kicked. Rolled onto his feet. Silas used Drake's own move against him, pinning Drake beneath him with his hind legs.

Defending himself, fighting with every last ounce of strength in his body, Drake snapped as Silas lowered himself over him.

...

Emelia couldn't watch, yet she couldn't tear her eyes away.

Mere seconds ago, Drake had the upper hand in the fight against his psychotic brother, but things had soured so quickly. He'd been bitten, though Emelia felt the pain as if she was the one who'd had Silas's fangs thrashing in her neck. Drake had lost so much blood, but Emelia felt the effects. She was woozy, her head light, her heart thumping in a hot, wild rush.

Silas rammed Drake to the ground and pinned him. Emelia felt the pain of the bites stinging through her body. Could taste the metallic flavor of Drake's blood as if it was on her tongue.

She could sense Drake's strength waning.

As Silas took a second and third bite out of Drake's neck, Emelia felt a surge of strength unlike anything she'd felt before. Her blood flushed differently through her veins. Her vision cleared to the point she could see air particles floating through the room and dust bunnies settling on the tables.

It wasn't the physical changes that had Emelia bursting through the ropes on her wrists and ankles. It was the pure, fiery flood of *wrath* coursing through her.

Time slowed to an impossible halt.

Anger seeped from her pores. Skin shrank over her bones. Her teeth ached, elongated, stretching her gums and brushing against her lips. Her muscles and tendons tightened into knots, shaking and trembling from the sheer force of her transformation. Clothes shed from Emelia's body as her back arched, and she dropped to all fours. Sleek, white fur flattened across her skin, and her gaze sharpened on Silas.

Hearing her approach, Silas stopped his assault on Drake and craned his neck around to meet her gaze. She was hurting where Drake hurt, feeling more powerful than ever, and hungry for blood.

Instead of attacking her, as Emelia expected, Silas backed away. She continued to stalk forward as he retreated, the excitement of the hunt fueling her on. She wanted him to run so she could follow. She wanted to taunt him, challenge him to get away from her. She felt unusually cocky—odd considering she hadn't tested out her wolf body yet.

Then Silas went and did the unthinkable. He lowered his muzzle to the floor in a mock bow.

What the hell?

Disappointed she wouldn't get the chase she craved, Emelia stopped over Drake's slumped body, her breath coming out in hard pants. Although Drake wasn't moving, he was alive; she could sense his heartbeat as if it were her own. How long he'd be alive was another question entirely. He'd already lost a lot of blood.

Get up, Drake.

Emelia eyed Silas carefully. His inky black fur and his dark, soulless eyes. Could he understand her if she told him to get the hell out of her bar and never return?

A growl tickled Emelia's belly, reverberated through her chest and escaped out her lips.

Silas raised his snout off the floor, stared deep into Emelia's eyes, and lunged for her throat. In a single, adrenaline-sparked move, Emelia clawed at Silas's jaw, sending him careering to the floor. His massive body slid along the hardwood and knocked into the wall. He hit so hard, the dartboard above his head rattled and shook, dislodged from its hook and toppled onto his head.

Confused, Emelia stared at the damage she'd created from a single swipe of her paw. Silas was bloody. Staring at her in shock and covered in darts and a busted board. Where Silas had hit the wall, there was an enormous hole.

She was strong. More powerful than she could've imagined.

Giving a solid shake, Silas clambered to his feet, the hair on the back of his neck rising into in a spiny black mohawk.

Don't die on me, Drake. I need you.

As if her silent plea awoke something inside him, Drake twitched, moved his feet beneath him, and stood beside her. Fury emanated from his body in hot surges, rippling on the air. The weakness Emelia had felt before was gone. In its place was barely controlled rage bubbling beneath the surface, ready to explode.

Through the haze of what was happening—the sensory overload stemming from her transition, Drake's anger, the rumble coming from Silas's chest—streaks of pride tinseled through Emelia's system. It felt good. Vibrant. It felt…*right.*

Drake marched forward, one slow paw hitting the hardwood, blood trickling down his legs. Emelia followed, feeling Drake's unbridled fury as her own. Step by step they closed in on Silas.

They created a united front. Stronger together. Never to be separated again.

As Drake growled, vibrating the floor beneath their feet, Silas's shoulders gave a hard twitch. His muzzle quirked and his gaze shifted to the door as a horde of howling packmates burst through, ripping it off its hinges. They corned Silas, bumped into him with their massive chests, and brought him to his belly with brute force.

Reinforcements had arrived.

Mr. Bloomfield strode through the door in their wake, dressed in a suit and tie as if he'd stepped from a board meeting into the fray. "Silas Wilder, you're under arrest for attempting to murder Drake Wilder, Alpha to the Seattle wolf pack, and Emelia Wilder, his mated female."

Silas whimpered against the ground as the wolves towered over him smashed him into the floor. There was nothing Silas could do. There were too many packmates, and they moved like an angry mob, swallowing everything in their wake.

So this was the pack family that Drake had told her about. They really did stand up for one another, didn't they? She'd never felt more relieved, or more protected, in all her life.

As Mr. Bloomfield and the packmates escorted Silas out the broken door, Drake crumbled. It'd been too much. He'd challenged Silas and fought at Emelia's side when he didn't have the strength to do either.

Emelia knelt over Drake and nudged him with her nose. Sighing into a full body shudder, Drake opened his eyes. They were soft black, warm and tender, piercing Emelia's heart. He shifted back to human form. Right beneath her legs. Naked and shivering, Drake reached up and brushed his hand down the slope of her face. Even through her fur, she could feel the pads on his fingers, the warmth of his palm, and the love behind his touch.

"Hello beautiful," Drake said, smiling. His wounds healed right before her eyes. His skin went from bloody to pink, his tissue from marred to bronze, sculpted muscle. "You're magnificent, though I didn't doubt you'd be amazing in this form, too."

Emelia nudged his palm, letting a little whimper escape

her chest. How did she shift back? Would she be stuck this way for the length of the full moon?

"An ambulance is on the way," Mr. Bloomfield said from the doorway. "Are you all right? Do you need anything?"

Drake stroked Emelia's nose, and scrubbed the fur behind her ears. "I've got everything I need right here."

"Don't need to tell me twice." Mr. Bloomfield left the bar as sirens wailed in the distance.

"I never thought I'd get to see you again." Drake stroked Emelia's fur, her chest. She could sense his strength returning each passing second. "I'm so sorry about what happened between us. I was beyond stupid. I should've never bought that bar behind your back and I should've supported you in this. That was wrong, so wrong. I should have followed you out that door."

No, she shouldn't have left in the first place.

"Don't do that," he said. "None of the blame is yours."

He could read her thoughts! She wasn't sure how or why the concept came easier to her now—perhaps it was because now that she'd shifted she could easily see herself as a part of his pack. Whatever the reason, Emelia's chest warmed. She'd done it. She'd shifted. And everything was going to be okay.

"I was wrong to try to convince you to get rid of this place," he said. "It's a part of you…you love it…which means I love it, too."

Emelia's heart overflowed, melting with joy. She'd thought that giving up the Knight Owl meant that she would be giving up her dream, her independence, and a little part of herself in the process. She'd always been the queen of overreaction and had blown things way out of proportion. To top off her ridiculousness, she'd fallen for a businessman… and had gotten mad at him when he talked business.

"I'll never try to force you into something again," he said, stroking her belly. "You can drive your Civic, work late hours here, and we can live wherever you want."

She really didn't care where she lived, as long as it was at his side. She never wanted to leave him again. How would they work out the fact that she'd run the Knight Owl and he'd run Wilder Financial? They'd still work in different worlds, wouldn't they? Is that what she wanted?

"I've already thought about that. I brought something for you that might help," he said, sliding from beneath her. He strode to where his shredded pants lay in a heap on the floor and dug around in his pocket. "Here," he said, straightening a piece of paper and holding it out in front of her.

What was it? She couldn't tell.

"It's your two-week notice. I don't want my wife, my soul mate, and my life partner working as my personal secretary. It's important that you see yourself how I see you: as my equal."

Oh, Drake. She was never cut out for the secretary gig. But now, when she was faced with the concept of leaving, she wasn't sure. It'd be nice to see him every day. To work alongside him.

"Then you will," Drake said, addressing her concerns. "Stand beside me as you did just now. Work alongside me. Be my partner in every sense of the word. I didn't realize it before, but if we mixed my business sense with your personal flair, we just might take Seattle by storm."

Emelia's heart went light. She quivered with the desire to kiss him, to feel his lips on hers. As she pinched her eyes shut, thinking about Drake and the future they'd have together, her body trembled and her skin heated sun-scorching hot. She shifted back to human form and jumped into Drake's arms.

He dropped the paper to the ground, cradled her head against him, and spun her around. "You did it," he said. "You figured out how to change back on your own."

"I just thought of you." She kissed him openmouthed

and slipped her tongue past his lips. Their mouths moved in a dance she didn't want to end. When Drake pulled back to get some air, Emelia said, "For a second there, I thought Silas was going to run from the fight. I thought he was going to back down."

"He realized the bond between us made us stronger. It made *you* stronger." Drake massaged her back, soothing away the worry and stress.

"But how's that possible? I mean, you guys are three hundred years old and I just learned how to shift. I'm a baby, or a pup, or whatever you'd call it."

His hand brushed her cheek. "Newly transitioned werewolves are uncharacteristically strong for the first hundred years of their life. Mesh that with being mated to me, and you're pretty special."

"You mean that I'm stronger because I've bonded with you?"

"You're my Luminary. There's a piece of you in me, and a piece of me in you. That gives you strength he could never understand."

"So it's over?" She dared to breathe deep.

"It's over." He kissed her. "I'm so glad you're all right."

"You're heaven-sent." Her heart hammered wildly. "But aren't you even a little upset about losing your father's estate to Silas?"

"I have you," Drake said. "It's all I want, and all I need. Besides, we didn't lose everything. We still have this place and Wilder Financial."

"Yeah," she said, realizing that he put the Knight Owl before his own business. It was actually going to work. They'd be happy, blissfully in love. "And we've got seven hundred years to be together. It still won't be long enough, but I'll take it."

Chapter Twenty-Two

CHRISTMAS DAY, ONE MONTH LATER

"Watch your step," Drake said, leading Emelia down the long, winding hall in the basement of his Seattle mansion.

Their *home*, she corrected, smiling inside.

The blindfold covering Emelia's eyes slipped a bit, but didn't give away whatever Drake was hiding. "The last time you blindfolded me it didn't go over too well," she said. "You sure you want to do this?"

"The last time I blindfolded you, I was a jackass." Drake guided her around a corner. "Thanks to you, I've thoroughly learned my lesson."

Stealing behind her, Drake looped his arms around Emelia's waist and tugged her against him. One step at a time, he led her into a room that smelled sweetly of vanilla and wine.

The wine cellar.

"Okay," he said, excitement lacing his voice. "You can look."

Emelia yanked the blindfold down and gasped. He'd turned the wine cellar into a romantic sanctuary, with a plush red blanket strewn on the floor, pillows leaning against the wine racks, and tea light candles flickering in the dark. There had to be hundreds of tiny lights scattered on the marble-topped tables, the hardwood floor, and the wooden ledge of the rack.

"It's beautiful," she whispered, leaning her head back on Drake's chest. "Thank you."

"Merry Christmas." He spun her around, keeping her tucked against his body, and caught her mouth. He embraced her full-bodied, hip to hip, mouth to mouth, dizzying her as his tongue swept past her lips. The kiss buzzed down to Emelia's toes—she'd never tire of the feelings Drake gave her.

She pulled back, gazing deep into her husband's eyes. He was her greatest wish…one she didn't think she'd ever receive. He was everything she never knew she wanted. "Merry Christmas to you, too."

"I thought we could exchange presents down here, before dinner."

"Okay," she said, unsure how Drake would respond when she gave him his gift. Luckily, she'd brought his gift with her.

"I've wanted to give this to you for a while." He dug around in the pocket of his blazer and pulled out a small box wrapped in sparkly silver wrapping, tied with a fluffy red bow. "But I thought tonight would be perfect. Do you realize we met almost two months ago today?"

Her insides tingled as she took the box and twirled it in her hand. "Drake…"

"Open it."

She untied the bow and let it fall, then tore through the wrapping. A black velvet box remained in the palm of her hand. She didn't want to get her hopes up, but Emelia knew what came in tiny black velvety boxes. Hands shaking, Emelia unhinged the lid and opened it. Her eyes met Drake's as tears began to fall.

"Drake, it's…it's beautiful." Her throat constricted. She couldn't speak.

"Do you really like it?"

The ring was big and sparkling and the exact opposite of what she would've picked for herself. A two-carat round diamond rose from the center of the ring and was surrounded by brilliant diamond clusters that wrapped around the band. It was breathtaking. The fact that he'd picked it for her, that he'd envisioned this ring on her finger when he perused hundreds of other rings, made Emelia's heart skip a beat.

When her eyes met Drake's again, he was kneeling in front of her. The sight almost buckled her.

"I know it's not something you would normally wear," he said, "but I couldn't take my eyes off of it, just like I couldn't take my eyes off of you the first time we met. From the first moment I met you, I've been completely, insanely captivated by your radiance."

Stomach in her throat, Emelia gazed at the ring. It was elaborate, and greater than her wildest dreams. It was *Drake*.

Holding her hand, Drake took the ring and poised it at the tip of her finger. "This ring is a promise of my love to you, Emelia. It's a symbol of my unending love, and my desire to make you happy until the end of your days."

As he slipped the ring on her finger, Emelia choked back tears. The ring fit snugly. Perfectly. When she held up her hand to see the diamond sparkle, she saw Drake. A part of him fitting perfectly on her finger, as he fit perfectly in her heart and in her life.

"It's perfect. I love it," she breathed, coiling her arms around his neck. "I love you."

"I love you ten times more." He stood and enveloped her in a heart-tingling embrace. "And I have one more surprise for you."

"More?" She couldn't handle more. Drake had already given her everything she'd ever wanted.

Picking up an opened bottle of Château Lafite from the wine barrel beside them, Drake poured two glasses. "A toast…using the wine that started it all."

Emelia laughed, eyeing the bottle, remembering how bitter she'd been that night at the party. "That's so sweet."

Drake offered Emelia the fuller of the two glasses. She took it, tasting the wine's mint aroma before a drop of it passed her lips. Its aroma was robust without being overpowering. She swirled the dark liquid around the bottom and wondered how she'd tell Drake that she didn't want a single drink of it.

"To the past, present, and future," he said, clinking his glass against hers.

"To our future," Emelia said, and watched him tip back the glass.

When he noticed she hadn't drunk anything, Drake said, "What's wrong?"

"I'm not drinking tonight." She tried to keep her thoughts quiet so he wouldn't read them.

"Come on, Emie, it's Christmas. Have a drink with me."

"Well, that's part of my present to you," she whispered.

His eyebrows hitched as confusion set in. "You're staying sober…as a gift to me?"

Slowly, she brought her hand to her stomach. "I'm not supposed to drink in my condition."

"In your—your what?" His eyes went wide as a smile teased the corners of his full lips. "Are you pregnant?"

She nodded, bursting. "Four weeks. I know it's early, but I've taken, like, ten tests and they all came out positive so…" She couldn't hide her elation. Could Drake see her glowing? "Merry Christmas!"

"Emelia!" Drake swept her into his arms and swung

her around, then stopped as if he realized he could hurt her. "That's great—that's amazing, I'm—I'm going to be a father!" He dropped to his knees, wrapped his arms around her hips, and kissed her stomach through her sweater. "Hear that, little one? I'm your father."

Emelia swooned, brushing her hands through Drake's dark hair. Would their baby have hair like his? Coarse and thick? Or would its hair be blond and wispy like hers? Would their baby's eyes be wild and blue or dark and mysterious? She couldn't wait to find out.

"I'm going to love you more than anyone else on this earth," Drake whispered against her. "Well, I'll love you and your mother equally. She's a very special woman, your mother," he said, "and I'll be right here to make sure you treat her right."

Her heart exploded, right then and there.

Drake rose to his feet and planted a kiss on Emelia's lips that spoke to her soul. They'd be together now and always.

As Drake pulled away, brushing his hands lovingly down Emelia's cheeks, she sensed a mild wave of panic brewing within him.

"What is it?" she asked.

"I might be jumping the gun, but do you need to sit down? I mean, what do you need? I want to make this pregnancy as smooth as possible for you. Do you want to find someone to take over some of the workload at the office? Or maybe hire someone to take over extra duties at the Knight Owl?"

"No," Emelia laughed. "I'm fine. I can do everything that I could do yesterday. At some point I think I'll probably need to stop working such late hours at the office with you, but I can't cut back, not yet, anyway. There's something I have to find first."

"Something you have to *find*? What are you talking about?" His hand brushed down her back, and stopped above the round of her backside. His touch warmed her, tingling her in places he'd just visited a few hours ago.

"When I first started working at Wilder Financial," she said, "there were some important documents that I...um, accidentally shredded that I need to locate in the computer system, reprint, and file."

"That was *you*?" He spanked her playfully. "What a bad secretary you are."

She smiled. "I'd like to make it up to you."

"Now we're talking." He kissed her, pulled back the collar of her sweater, and continued scattering kisses across her shoulder. "If you work your shift really hard, I think you just might make Secretary of the Year."

"Mr. Drake Wilder, I do believe that's something I would say!" Emelia laughed at the thought that she was rubbing off on him. *What would his business associates think?*

He smiled, a devious twinkle in his eye. "Frankly, my dear, I don't give a howl."

Acknowledgments

First and foremost, I have to thank the savvy ladies at Entangled Publishing. I'm so thrilled to be a part of your publishing family. Liz Pelletier and Kaleen Harding, my editors: you two are brilliant beyond words. Thank you.

As always, thanks and hugs to Nalini Akolekar, my lovely agent, for knowing what I want for my career before I do. For the record, you were right about…well, everything.

My work would be unintelligible mush without the input of my fabulous critique partners and early readers: Aggie Smith, AJ Larrieu, Lisa Sanchez, Vanessa Kier, and Virna DePaul. Thanks ladies, from the bottom of my heart.

Hugs and kisses to my family and friends who help out when deadlines loom and the words just won't flow without a last-minute plotting session. You keep me on track. You keep me sane and make me laugh until my cheeks hurt. I don't know where I'd be without you.

To Justin, Kelli, and Gavin: you three are my everything. Love, love, love, and heartfelt thanks for supporting me while I chase down my dream.

About the Author

New York Times and *USA TODAY* bestselling author Kristin Miller writes sweet and sassy contemporary romance and paranormal romance of all varieties. Kristin has degrees in psychology, English, and education, and taught high school and middle school English before crossing over to a career in writing. She lives in Northern California with her alpha male husband and their two children. She loves chocolate way more than she should and the gym less. You can usually find her in the corner of a coffee shop, laptop in front of her and mocha in hand, using the guests around her as fuel for her next book.

Don't miss the rest of the Seattle Wolf Pack series

FOUR WEDDINGS AND A WEREWOLF

SO I MARRIED A WEREWOLF

Also by Kristin Miller

THE WEREWOLF WEARS PRADA

BEAUTY AND THE WEREWOLF

WHAT A WEREWOLF WANTS

Discover more paranormal romance titles from Entangled...

The Alpha's Temporary Mate
a *Fated Match* novel by Victoria Davies

Witch and matchmaker, Chloe Donovan, takes pride in helping her clients find their happy endings. But when werewolf alpha and millionaire playboy Kieran Clearwater stalks into her office, she may have finally met the one man she can't help. For Kieran, love is a weakness he can't afford, but he coerces Chloe to be his fake girlfriend. While these two burn hot when they're together, behind-the-scenes politics work to rip them apart.

Ghost of You
a *Phantoms* novel by Kelly Moran

It's no secret amongst the *Phantoms* crew that lead investigator Sammy Hanesworth pretty much hates psychologist Cain McClutchen. The tension between them is taut with dislike…and unexpected attraction. The Nebraskan site they're investigating is more than creepy. It's also Sammy's hometown. As the sinister presence makes itself known, Sammy finds herself turning to the last person she ever expected—Cain. But nothing will prepare them for the evil they are about to face…

LONE WOLFE PROTECTOR
a *Wolfe Creek* novel by Kaylie Newell

When Maggie Sullivan comes to Wolfe Creek, determined to find out why her best friend vanished one fog-shrouded night a year ago, seasoned sheriff's deputy Koda Wolfe reluctantly agrees to help. Soon he's compelled to protect Maggie from herself, his family's ancient curse, and a killer who could strike again. The nights heat up in more ways than one as Maggie and Koda begin a fiery relationship. But as they delve deeper into the disappearance, the eerie woods come alive with secrets bound to tear them apart. And someone is watching their every move.

LIONS, TIGERS, AND SEXY BEARS, OH MY!
a novel by Candace Havens

Everything about runaway heiress Ainsley McLeon screamed trouble. Yet sexy, stoic bar owner Luc couldn't deny the instant connection he felt to the tempting stranger. Ainsley traveled with her own emotional baggage and there was no way she'd fall for the bear-tempered Luc…no matter how many passionate nights she spent in his bed or how safe she felt in his muscular arms. Can these two opposites find love in the middle of a blizzard, or will Luc's darker side and Ainsley's past catch up with them?